THE RETREAT

NICOLA MARSH

For fellow readers who grew up devouring haunting tales by Victoria Holt and Daphne du Maurier. It's been way too many years since I read their page-turners. Time to rectify that.

You can stay, but you may never leave...

For guests who spend a week at Arcania, a wellness retreat in the Outer Banks for those wanting to digitally detox, the gothic mansion is a welcome haven. Others aren't so lucky.

When Lucy's mother dies unexpectedly and a mysterious Viking tattoo reveals a link to Arcania, Lucy books a week at the retreat. Cora Medville, the owner, seems welcoming enough, but soon the creepy house and its inhabitants are urging Lucy to flee, or risk dying like some before her.

Four decades earlier, runaway Cora is smitten by Arcania and the dashing owner Harlan. Craving a sense of belonging, she finds it with her new family and their majestic mansion.

But when residents start disappearing and she learns the terrifying truth, who can she trust?

How far will she go to protect Arcania's sordid secrets?

PROLOGUE

I never should've come here.

Searching for answers to questions better left unasked has put me in danger. The evil is palpable, oozing from the walls, permeating the air like the stench from the swamp surrounding Arcania.

This wellness retreat, welcoming on the outside, malevolent on the inside, isn't a place where busy people come to digitally detox.

Some come here and die.

Overly dramatic? Maybe. But I've witnessed firsthand the changes in fellow guests and it's not pretty.

Fellow lost souls searching for... something.

Finding devastation instead.

Looking in a mirror and not liking what they see.

Reflective contemplation that unearths guilt and grief and unspeakable horror.

I'm grieving. It's eating away at me. But I won't let them know. The inhabitants of Arcania will use it against me. I have to be smarter.

Because if they discover who I am, I'll never make it out of this sinister hellhole alive.

CHAPTER 1

LUCY

I'm at work in the smallest library in Manhattan, hiding away in my favorite carrel on my lunch break, when my cell vibrates on the desk. It nudges a red pen I've been using to edit my measly word count and I watch it roll off the desk. Anything to distract from the procrastination I've become so good at.

What made me think I could write a book? I'm a librarian, surrounded by books every day, and when I'm not shelving, cataloguing, and assisting fellow book lovers or inquiring minds, I'm curled up in an armchair at home reading. That should be enough for me but no, I had to let the kernel of an idea for a young adult paranormal novel grow until I couldn't ignore it.

I've told no one, not even Mom. She'd be supportive, but until I know I can do it—increasingly unlikely as the blank page at the start of chapter four has taunted me for three days in a row—I'm not telling anyone.

My cell vibrates again, and this time I glance at the screen. I don't get a lot of calls. Mom and work are in my contacts, that's it. It's lame not to be dating at twenty-five, but after my last lackluster relationship that lasted all of six weeks, I'm focusing on myself for a change.

The cell continues to shimmy across the desk and I pick it up. It's not Mom and I don't recognize the number. Like libraries the world over, talking is frowned upon unless in designated areas, so I glance sideways, relieved no one's at the neighboring carrels. Maybe it's my muse calling, and it's time I answered? With a wry smile at my lame joke, I accept the call.

"Hi, this is Lucy Phillips." I leave off the standard 'Lower Manhattan Library, how can I help you?' that's become so ingrained I'm sure I recite it in my sleep.

"Ms. Phillips, this is Officer Lewis of the NYPD. I'm at the front desk. Could I speak with you, please?"

I ease the cell away from my ear in surprise. What would the police want with me? I'm the most boring person in this vibrant, eclectic city. I work, I pay my taxes, I live in a brownstone with my mom. I'm not on any social media; my otherwise calm mother got heated about that when drilling the importance of keeping a low profile online when I hit my teens. I attributed her paranoia to her agoraphobia, but I agreed regardless because I'm not a fan of parading my life online for all to see.

Not that I had much of a life in my teens: I may not fear people like Mom but being a quiet book nerd didn't exactly make me popular. But at least these days it pays the bills.

So yeah, I'm boring. I spend my life here, at home, or walking in Central Park because I feel like it's a writerly thing to do: to gain perspective, people watch, store away snatches of conversation for realistic dialogue.

"Call me Lucy."

It's an inane response, and Officer Lewis clears his throat. "It's important we speak immediately."

In that moment, the enormity of the call hits me. This can't be about our resident book thief who's accumulated eighteen months' worth of fines.

This must be about Mom.

"Is my mother okay?"

His pause is ominous, and the fine hairs on my arms snap to attention.

Before he can respond, I say, "I'll be there in a minute," and hang up, scoop my notebook and pens into my satchel, and break into a half-jog.

I spy the officer as I round the carrels. He's not alone. A female officer is with him and the moment our gazes lock, her expression of practiced sympathy makes my stomach drop.

My steps slow, keeping pace with the pounding of my heart as I approach. Dread makes my palms clammy and I surreptitiously swipe them down the side of my denim skirt. The gesture doesn't go unnoticed as both officers watch me do it, almost as if they don't want to look me in the eye.

That's when I notice the front desk is empty. Glenda never leaves her post, ever, unless for scheduled breaks, and even then she's vigilant about someone covering for her to the extent she draws up a roster every Monday. Her absence reinforces what I already know deep in my gut.

The news the officers need to impart isn't good.

When I reach them, Officer Lewis says, "Is there somewhere we can talk more privately?"

"We have rooms reserved for students." My voice quavers as I point toward four conference-style rooms to our left.

He nods, as the female officer introduces herself. "I'm Officer Helsham."

"Pleased to meet you," I say, a polite, rote response when on the inside I'm a mess. Every instinct is screaming at me to run and hide in the stacks, far from the bad news the officers are likely to impart.

We don't speak as we head toward the first vacant room, and once Officer Lewis closes the door, Officer Helsham gestures to a chair. "Have a seat."

When I don't move, my panicked gaze swinging between them, she exchanges a quick glance with her male counterpart before continuing. "I'm afraid we have some bad news for you, Lucy."

I collapse into the nearest chair, my legs wobbly and my trepidation increasing. My satchel clangs against the metal leg of the chair and it opens, sending a pack of colorful tabs I use for annotation and several pens rolling beneath the table. I don't care. My gaze rivets to Office Helsham, who sits opposite me. She's too close, like she expects I'll sway or faint when she tells me what's happened.

"Your mother has been involved in a vehicular accident, and I'm afraid she didn't survive."

I bark out a laugh, and both officers rear back in surprise. "There must be some mistake. My mom doesn't own a car, and she never gets into one. She barely sets foot out of our home because she's agoraphobic. So it's not possible she's been involved in a car accident."

The officers exchange another of those loaded glances before Officer Helsham says, "We're sorry to say a bus hit your mother and she didn't survive the impact."

My blood runs cold, thick, and sluggish in arteries and veins that constrict with shock, making me lightheaded. My instant dismissal when they first told me gives way to doubt. Mom rarely leaves our brownstone, but it has happened before. On those occasions, she cited medical treatment as the reason and I hoped she'd improve enough to make it a regular occurrence. If she set foot outside a few times, maybe she'd learn she had nothing to fear. But she didn't change, and I grew accustomed to keeping her company at home rather than going out. We were a couple of hermits, comfortable in our environment, and the fact I'm using 'were', past tense, in my mind means the news is sinking in.

My quiet, staid, sensible mom is dead.

My throat tightens, and tears burn my eyes as I begin to shake. My teeth clatter and Office Helsham reaches out to place a comforting hand on my forearm.

"I'm sorry to ask this of you, Lucy, but we'll need you to come with us to the Medical Examiner's office now and confirm her identity."

I stare at the policewoman, unseeing, her face distorted by my tears as the sobs welling in my chest burst forth and I'm ugly crying, hunched over, wrapping my arms around my middle, wishing this nightmare would end.

The next two hours are a blur. Accompanying the police to the M.E.'s office, refusing to peer through the glass at the sheet-covered body on a steel gurney, being led into the room by the two officers bracing me either side, their grip firm on my elbows but useless against my overwhelming grief as the sheet is tugged back and I glimpse the familiar face of my mom. She's surprisingly bruise-free and I'm glad her body took the brunt of the impact, because I would've hated seeing her mangled. Her expression is serene, like she's taking a nap, and I almost reach out to give her a little shake to wake up.

As I'm being led from the room, an examiner lifts the sheet from her feet, checks the toe tag and scribbles something on a document. Confirmation that my life as I know it is over.

I'm alone.

We have no family. Mom hated talking about her past, which included my father and her parents, and would almost hyperventilate if I probed, so I gave up asking in my teens. I've never understood why I have my father's surname if she hated him so much and I didn't like having a different surname to her, particularly at high school where bullies latched onto anything to make my life hell. Online searches proved futile too and I often wonder if she'd changed our names because she was running from something.

Now I'll never know.

I stumble and the officers tighten their grip, and as I glance at my mother's lifeless body for the last time, I see it.

A tattoo on the sole of her right foot.

My pristine, strait-laced mom, who never drank, smoked, and always abhorred tattoos of any kind, has a strange nautical compass branded on her body.

"Is something wrong?" Officer Helsham asks, her tone soft and solicitous, and I shake my head.

What can I say? That everything is wrong and even in death, my secretive mom is surprising me?

"We'll take you home now," Officer Lewis says, and I nod.

Shock is giving way to fatigue and I'm exhausted to my bones. I crave the quiet of our apartment, the solitude to process and grieve in peace.

But while I want to crawl into bed once I'm home and the officers leave—after pressing a therapist's business card into my hand—I don't. Every time I close my eyes I see my mom's ashen face and that weird tattoo, so I do a quick sketch from memory—eight compass points ending in odd little pitchfork squiggles, surrounded by double circles and an archaic alphabet—and do an online search.

As I scroll through images of various compasses on my computer screen, I see what I'm looking for in the second row, far right. The same emblem Mom had tattooed on her foot. It's a Viking compass, a *vegvisir*, translated to mean a signpost or way finder, an Icelandic magical stave.

I peer closer. My sensible mother would be the least likely person to believe in magic. Heck, she wouldn't watch anything remotely otherworldly on TV and scoffed at my choice of paranormal fantasy reading.

So what was she doing with a magical symbol combining runes from the Old Norse alphabet tattooed on her body and hiding it from me her entire life?

I used to tease her about wearing socks even in summer and she always said they comforted her; that keeping her feet warm made her feel safe. I dismissed it as one of her many quirks, but now I'm wondering why she needed to hide a symbol that represented strength, guidance, and protection?

What had my mom run from in the past?

As I click on the symbol to do a more extensive search, I spot the compass again but this time it's emblazoned on a sign outside an aging mansion. Curious, I follow the website link to Arcania, a wellness retreat in the Outer Banks region of North Carolina for those who want to digitally detox.

I enlarge the photo of the mansion and an unexpected shiver tiptoes from the nape of my neck to my lower back. It's nothing overt, but the place has an eerie air that creeps me out.

Irrationally, I shut the website down and continue my

search to see if my mom's tattoo is used as a logo for any other places, but there's nothing.

Arcania is the only link to Mom's tattoo.

It's silly, wanting to delve into something Mom has kept hidden for twenty-five years and could lead nowhere. But I've always been curious about my past and having something to focus on will ease the unrelenting sorrow making the simple act of breathing difficult.

I blame the grief clouding my judgement when I do the unthinkable and make a booking to spend a week at Arcania.

CHAPTER 2
CORA

T HEN

I SHOULD'VE KNOWN TURNING eighteen on Friday the thirteenth would be momentous. Then again, considering what I'd escaped from and gone through to get here, I deserve a change in luck.

I can't remember when I fled Miami. Two days ago? Three? Changing buses frequently and barely sleeping for fear of someone snatching my duffel out of my hands means I stagger off the bus in Nag's Head bleary-eyed but ecstatic.

I've done it.

I've escaped.

The Outer Banks of North Carolina may not have been my final destination when I left Florida because I didn't know where I wanted to go, but it will be my new home. As far from my mom's sleazy boyfriends as I can get.

Anonymity is guaranteed in a town where nobody knows me. It's a heady feeling when I've had to look over my shoulder and barricade my bedroom door for the last few years.

As the bus pulls away, I spy a small cafe on the other side of the road. It's deserted, but the tantalizing aroma of frying onions beckons and reminds me of how long since I ate an apple about ten hours ago.

My stomach growls as I enter the cafe. It's deserted and some of the tension holding my shoulders rigid for the last seventy-two hours since I escaped eases. A girl about my age is behind the counter, scrolling through her cell and I glimpse an old guy at a stove through a long rectangular window behind her.

"Hey," I say, quickly scanning the chalkboard menu above her head, relieved when I see I can get a hotdog for a few dollars. I've been scrimping and saving for nine months, ever since the first time that creep Mom loves lay a hand on my butt, but my meager money stash won't last forever. I need to find a job ASAP. "Can I get a hotdog, please?"

The girl doesn't glance up from her cell and shouts, "One hot dog, Digby."

Digby salutes to no one in particular and returns to his frying onions. I grab a soda from the fridge and place it on the counter a little harder than intended, and the girl finally looks up.

Her eyes are freaky, one hazel, the other blue. "You're new here."

I don't feel like making chit chat, but she may know where I can find a job so it pays to be nice. "Yeah, just got into town."

"Tourist?" Her eyebrow rises, the ring piercing it tugging on the skin.

"No. I want to stay for a while. Find a job."

"Who'd want to live here?" Her eyes narrow as she looks me up and down, as if doubting my mental capacity. "This place is for rich folk and tourists."

And for people like me seeking blessed anonymity.

"So you don't know of any work?"

"Nope. But there are plenty of shops and restaurants if you head into town. Check there."

"Thanks."

Digby gives a high-pitched whistle signaling the hotdog is ready as he slides it through the window from the kitchen. It's oozing ketchup, mustard and those aromatic onions and I salivate as I hand over my money, nod my thanks at the grouchy girl and take my hotdog and soda outside.

My duffel bumps my back and it's comforting, a reminder of how far I've come. I packed light, essentials only—underwear, five T-shirts, three pairs of jeans, two cotton dresses, socks, and toiletries—enough to get by on until I earn a wage.

It should terrify me that all my worldly possessions are in this duffel, but it doesn't. What I left behind, an oblivious, uncaring mother and her sleazy boyfriend, was far scarier.

There are three plastic tables beneath turquoise-striped umbrellas and matching chairs outside, and I choose the only table in the shade under an awning. I sit, place my food and drink on the table, and tuck my duffel between my feet. I'm almost faint with hunger and the first bite of the hotdog is heaven. The tang of mustard and the bitterness from the slightly charred onions makes my tastebuds dance and I literally groan and take another bite, wondering if Digby is a magician who puts secret sauce on this. I demolish it quickly, wishing I had the funds to stretch to another, and take a sip of soda when a shadow falls over me.

I shade my eyes and look up, trying not to react when the most gorgeous guy I've ever seen smiles. He's tall, broad-shouldered, and looks like he spends all day in the gym.

"Mind if I sit?" He points to the spare chair at my table and I nod before I can second-guess the wisdom of encouraging a stranger to join me. "You new in town?"

"Maybe," I say, wary yet intrigued.

The guy's a similar age to me, or maybe early twenties, and he's rich. I can tell by the logo on his navy polo and the expensive watch on his wrist. Plus he smells incredible, an intoxicating blend of sea and spice, and to smell that good, the aftershave must cost a bomb.

"I'm just asking because my folks run a bed and breakfast near here and lots of newbies stay there."

He's offhand, diffident, like he doesn't care if I'm listening or not, but I feel his eyes watching me. They're pale blue, like a washed-out sky, striking with a hint of something that has me on edge.

I should avoid strangers offering accommodation to girls sitting alone at roadside cafes at all costs, but I'm poor and desperate. What harm can it do to delve further?

"How far?"

"We're in Flotilla Firth, about fifty miles up the road. It's a tiny town and the folks who live at Arcania are basically the only inhabitants."

"Did you make up that name?"

"Which one?"

He smiles again and I swear my heart skips a beat. He has even white teeth that light up his face, and along with the clean-shaven square-cut jaw, high cheekbones, those peculiar eyes, and ruffled hair the color of burned caramel, he packs a punch.

"English was my favorite subject at school, so I know arcane means keeping a secret, and it makes me wonder what you're hiding at Arcania, but Flotilla Firth? Where the heck did that come from?"

He laughs, a deep, warm sound that washes over me like the sea in Miami on a summer's day. "Lots of ships, flotillas of them, wrecked off the coast near Arcania and the place is steeped in history. It's been in my family for generations." He taps the side of his nose and winks. "Maybe those secrets we keep involve buried treasure?"

I like his playfulness and relax a little. "If your family has lived there for so long you must be loaded, so why run a B&B?"

I glimpse respect in his gaze. "Because we also have the biggest organic farm in North Carolina and always need workers, so we offer free food and accommodation as an incentive. Working in the orchards is hard work and turnover is high, so it's good to offer a little extra."

This sounds too good to be true. I need a job and a place to stay, and here's this guy offering me both after I barely step off the bus. But I'm not an idiot. I'm not going anywhere with him until I find out if he's legit.

"Sounds like an interesting place." I stand, sling my bag over my shoulder, and place the hotdog wrapper and soda can in the nearby trash. "I just need to grab something inside and use the restroom. Back in a minute."

"Take your time. I'm not going anywhere."

That's what worries me—does he prey on all newbies

to town?—but heading back inside the cafe will give me a chance to slip out the side door if I need to escape. I barely set foot inside when the girl behind the counter says, "Harlan offering you a place to stay?"

I can't believe I don't even know his name. That's what happens when I'm stupidly drooling over his general dreaminess.

"Yeah. Does he do it to everyone?"

She shrugs, but I see her wistful gaze land on him outside. "If he's driving past and sees an out-of-towner, he'll stop to offer them accommodation."

"So he's not a serial killer?"

"Heck, no." But her glance slides away, like she's hiding something.

"But?"

She huffs out a sigh, like I'm bothering her. "There are rumors about Arcania being haunted. Stuff that kids scare each other about at campfires on the beach around here and have for decades. Probably nothing."

Once again, I get the feeling she's leaving something out, so I pin her with the killer stare I used on Mom's latest boyfriend when he accidentally on purpose caressed my boob, and the final straw that drove me to run away. "Tell me."

Her gaze flickers to Harlan again before she looks back at me. "Some say the Medvilles run a cult out there. That once people arrive at Arcania, they never want to leave."

"Maybe it's a great place to work and live?"

"Maybe." She shrugs. "Honestly? If Harlan offered me a place to stay, I'd be there in a heartbeat."

Discounting her crush, I say, "So everyone around here knows his family?"

She shoots me a 'duh' look. "They're the richest family

for hundreds of miles around here, so yeah, we know them."

Reassured I'm not at risk of being abducted into some nefarious house for runaways, I nod. "Thanks. Can I use your restroom?"

"Yeah. It's out the back."

As I head toward the side door, I feel Harlan watching me through the cafe's front window. My back tingles, like someone has run their fingers down my spine, and I give a little shake.

Lack of sleep is making me dramatic. With my limited funds, I can't afford to be choosy about where I stay and here's a nice guy who checks out, whose parents run a B&B, offering me a place for the night. And with a little luck, I can wangle a job working on their organic farm, too.

I'd be a fool to turn him down.

CHAPTER 3
LUCY

The moment I lay eyes on Arcania, I second-guess my decision to come. What am I hoping to find? An explanation why my mom had their logo tattooed on her foot and some nebulous link to a past I know nothing about?

It's ludicrous.

But it's also a distraction from my relentless grief. I've barely eaten the last two weeks, losing myself in the newest paranormal novels from my towering to be read pile and blasting music to detract from the oppressive silence.

That's the thing I miss most with Mom gone. She hated leaving the house, so when I got home from work she'd talk nonstop; often about inane stuff, anything from the latest reality TV dramas to an online chat forum for agoraphobes like her. I tuned her out sometimes because that's the thing about working in a library: I love the silence. I prefer it. So Mom's chatter got to me at times. Which means I lamented her loss a hundred times harder over the last few weeks when the quiet made me yearn for her even more.

The sun dips behind the house—more a mansion, with fifteen windows on each level across two floors—casting a mauve tinge over the whitewashed walls and turning the green trim a muddy brown. It's not as glamorous as it appears online, probably the result of some expensive photo doctoring software. In fact, an air of menace clings to the mansion at sunset, and as a soft breeze lifts the hair off the nape of my neck and trepidation tiptoes down my spine, I wonder if it's too late to leave.

As if sensing my reluctance to enter, a woman appears on a path to the right and waves. Casting a last wistful glance over my shoulder at the taxi that is almost out of view now, I clutch my satchel and wheel my suitcase toward her.

She moves fast, and with her feet hidden beneath a long white tunic that skims the ground, she gives the appearance of floating. My steps drag and when she reaches me, she flings her arms wide.

"Welcome to Arcania. You must be Lucy Phillips? We've been expecting you."

She speaks as fast as she moves, the words tumbling out of her mouth in excitement. "I'm Cora Medville, the owner of this little slice of heaven. I'm so happy you're here."

I wish I could say the same, but my doubts are overwhelming. What am I hoping to find? What will I do if I discover the truth about Mom's past? And the kicker, how will I survive with no internet for seven days?

Sensing my hesitation, she takes a step back to give me some space. "Digitally detoxing isn't for everyone but I can assure you that you'll leave here a different person."

"Right."

It's the first word I've uttered, and she appears taken aback, her hazel eyes narrowing slightly, studying me. "We don't ask you to hand over devices because you'll have no reception out here anyway. But if you need to contact anyone in an emergency, don't hesitate to reach out."

"Thanks," I say, and it comes out a tad squeaky courtesy of my throat constricting at the thought of having no one to contact now that Mom's gone.

"Let's get you checked in, then I'll have Spencer show you to your room."

I nod and fall into step beside her, lengthening my stride to keep up with her. At a guess, Cora is around sixty, but she appears a decade younger with her radiant skin, long blonde hair and clear blue eyes. The white tunic should've aged her. Instead, she looks like an angel.

I stub my toe on a cracked paver and stumble, pausing to let the initial pain pass. When I glance up, Cora's two feet in front of me, striding toward the house, and I see it.

The Viking compass, emblazoned on the back of her tunic in vivid turquoise, the same color as Mom's tattoo, and I'm catapulted back to that awful day in the medical examiner's office having to identify my mother.

Realizing I'm not following, she stops and glances over her shoulder. "Are you alright, dear?"

I nod, grief making breathing difficult. Focusing on the throb in my toe is almost a relief, a welcome distraction from a distinct urge to sink to my knees and bawl. "Stubbed my toe."

"Ouch. That always hurts."

I can't drag my eyes away from her back and she notices. "Our logo is something else, isn't it?"

"It's distinctive."

Beaming, she nods. "The only one of its kind. My husband's ancestors were from Iceland so you'll see a lot of Nordic influence in Arcania. We use Norse mythology and symbolism in a lot of our treatments too."

"I saw you have an extensive list on offer in your day spa."

I want to keep her talking about the logo but don't want to appear too eager. She's garrulous and if I gently probe for answers, there's less chance of her clamming up.

"Oh yes, it more than makes up for the lack of access to the precious social media apps so many who come here are addicted to."

I mumble an agreement and fall into step beside her, when she says, "I notice you aren't on any social media sites."

Surprised, I shoot her a sideways glance. Why would she look me up?

"No. I'm not interested in sharing my life with the world or seeing what an old classmate's dog has eaten for dinner."

She laughs. "Good for you. It's unusual, that's all."

For a moment, I wonder who's probing who for information, and I shrug. "I'm far from unusual. I'm more mundane."

"Then why are you here, Lucy?" Her curious gaze skewers me, like she can see straight to my soul. "If you're not online much, why do you need to detox?"

I almost snap 'mind your own business', but if this woman knows as much about Norse mythology as she proclaims, she may have answers about my mother.

Feeling increasingly out of my depth, I mumble, "I'm a librarian, so I'm online for work a lot."

"Ah, that explains it," she says, but it doesn't, because as she opens the front door and I catch my first jaw-dropping glimpse of Arcania's interior, I have a feeling Cora's watching me, waiting for me to slip up and reveal why I'm really here.

CHAPTER 4
CORA

T HEN

HARLAN HAS a flashy red convertible and I feel like I'm in a movie as he zooms along the highway toward Arcania.

"What brings you to the Outer Banks?" He asks, turning down the radio. Not that he needs to. Unlike most guys his age who'd be blasting rock, pop, or rap, he's listening to some New Age crap that sounds like waterfalls tumbling over rocks.

"I'm looking for a fresh start."

"How old are you?"

"Eighteen. How old are you?"

"Twenty-one."

We lapse into silence but it's short-lived when he asks, "Why aren't you in college?"

"Why aren't you?" I counter, though I know the answer. If his parents are rich and have owned Arcania for centuries, he doesn't need to study. He'll inherit the lot once his wealthy folks are gone.

"I've completed my bachelor's in economics."

I make a scoffing sound and he sniggers. "I don't like to brag, but I'm gifted. Finished school at fifteen, completed my degree last year."

"Good for you."

He laughs at my sarcasm. "Don't sweat it. College isn't for everyone."

He's got that right. I barely made it through high school, my focus on finishing so I could leave Miami and never look back.

I won't be missed. Mom barely acknowledged I existed over the years, her never-ending string of loser boyfriends taking all her attention. She worked as a receptionist at an attorney's office—ironic, because half the guys she dated probably needed a lawyer to keep them out of prison at one stage or another—so she earned enough to clothe and feed me, but that's where her mothering ended. When I hit my teens, we argued. A lot. She didn't like me criticizing her choice of companionship, I didn't like the way she couldn't see what was happening right under her nose when those sleazebags would look at me with lust in their eyes.

So I plotted and planned and waited until here I am, being interrogated by some rich jerk I have to play nice with, so I have a roof over my head until I find a job.

"I may not have gone to college, but I'm a fast learner," I say, hating how inferior he's making me feel. "Speaking of which, do you know of anyone who needs help around here?"

"You want a job?"

"Yeah." Like yesterday, considering my pitiful funds.

"One of our workers left unexpectedly last night, so

there's an opening. My folks will want to interview you, but I'll vouch for you."

I'm instantly on guard. He doesn't know me. Why would he put in a good word?

"Let me get this straight. Arcania houses newbies in town like me for free and you'll pay me to work there?"

If something sounds too good to be true, it usually is and despite my precarious position, I'm not an idiot. He's probably figured I'm a runaway and who knows what may happen if I trust him?

He gives me side eye. "Don't make it sound creepy. We're like a family at Arcania. Everyone loves it."

"Who's everyone?"

"As you know, my folks own it. Then there's Spencer and Daphne, who basically run the place, pseudo house-keepers, I guess. Spencer oversees the day to day running in the house, Daphne the kitchen. There's about twenty people working the orchard and staying long term at the moment, but more come and go."

"What about you? What do you do?"

"I'm a jack of all trades." His audible pride makes him sit taller. Conceited, much? "I do what needs to be done."

There's an undercurrent of something I can't put my finger on beneath his pride, but I'm distracted from asking because he slows the car, turns off the highway, and I get my first glimpse of Arcania.

It's spectacular and much bigger than I imagined. It's like the French provincial mansions Mom used to gush over on TV—symmetrical architecture, ivory brick exterior, steep roof, arched-top windows—but it's the size that impresses me. It's huge. I don't have time to count all the front windows before Harlan follows an unpaved road around the side of the house, and that's when I see where everyone lives. About fifteen massive tents circle a monstrous fire pit, but these are no ordinary tents. They look like those posh, glamping ones for people who want to try camping but hate the basics.

"Impressive, huh?"

"Yeah," I say, unable to subdue a tiny flicker of excitement. Living and working here would be great and to luck into it on my first day arriving in this place...my life has been crap to date, so maybe this is karma's way of finally giving me a break?

He parks the car, and we get out. He's staring at me with the oddest expression on his face, part-hope, part-creepy, and my excitement from a moment ago fades. What am I doing here? I don't know these people, and while the cafe girl might've vouched for this family, I hope I haven't fled one dire situation to another.

Sensing my distress, Harlan comes to stand next to me. "Don't be scared. I've got your back."

I bite back my first retort, "Why? You don't know me." Determined to show no fear, I square my shoulders and hoist my duffel higher. "If you could show me where I'm staying, that'll be great."

He casts me a glance I can't fathom before gesturing at the house. "Come this way."

"I'm staying in there?"

"Yeah. We reserve the tents for families and couples. Singles get a room inside."

I'm not sure whether to be relieved I'll be ensconced safely in the house or fearful: the bedroom doors better have locks.

"Your folks don't mind strangers living in their house?"

Though calling this mansion a house is like calling a mountain a molehill.

"They prefer it. It's too quiet when it's just the three of us."

"How long have they been doing this? Letting their workers stay rather than having them live offsite?"

"Since I went to college." He shrugs. "I guess they hated the silence when I wasn't around and found a way to fill it."

While their generosity is admirable, I still think it's weird. If I was this rich and lived in a place like this, I wouldn't want a bunch of nobodies traipsing through my house. Then again, maybe I'm selfish because I'm poor and have had to fight to protect everything I have, which isn't much.

"I'm sure they'll love to meet you." Harlan opens the unlocked front door and steps aside, gesturing me in.

Taking a deep breath, I enter, and a chill ripples over my bare arms, like someone has doused me in icy water.

I balk, resisting the urge to rub my arms, as the chill spreads from my arms to my torso and lower, until my legs wobble.

Every hair on my body is standing on end, a physiological alarm alerting me that something isn't right here.

"Everything okay?" His fingers graze the small of my back, a fleeting touch that should've reassured me. It doesn't.

I should leave. Turn around, march outside and not come back. I don't believe in places having an aura, but if I did, this one wouldn't be good.

But I have nowhere to go, it's late in the afternoon, and I'm exhausted from lack of sleep.

What harm can staying one night do?

CHAPTER 5
LUCY

Entering Arcania is like stepping into one of my favorite paranormal novels, heavy on the goth. The floors are polished parquet, a sweeping double staircase made from ornate black wrought iron filigree leads to the upper story, purple velvet drapes cover the windows, and crimson chaises are dotted around the foyer. Brass sconces set high on the walls cast a dim light over everything and there's a weird smell in the air, a hint of copper and brine that's inadequately masked by the air diffusers dispensing a vanilla fragrance. A brocade chair is tucked behind a mahogany desk in an alcove on the right, with a surprisingly modern computer on it.

"I'll check you in over there," Cora says, pointing at the desk. "What do you think of Arcania?"

For a wellness retreat that specializes in digital detox, I'd expected clean lines and modern architecture, so I don't think Cora wants to know what I really think. The overall atmosphere is cloying, the decor better suited to a hotel that promotes ghost tours. Not that I believe in them. Considering how much I miss Mom I wish I did. This seems like the perfect place to reach out to relatives beyond the grave.

"It's got a distinct old-world charm."

"Thanks, we love it." Her eyes glow with fervor. "I've tried to preserve the history of the place here in the lobby, but you'll find the rooms and day spa are ultra-modern." Maintaining the history explains the gothic vibe. "Please, let's get you settled."

As I sit opposite Cora and she types something, presumably my name, on the keyboard, I have a chance to study her. With her unlined skin and glossy dark blonde hair lightly streaked with gray, she has an ageless quality I envy. Mom was like that too, though she'd been dying her hair auburn for as long as I can remember. I always thought the red washed her out, but she religiously touched up her color every eight weeks.

The phone rings, a mini-modern switchboard showing where the call's coming from that's oddly out of place with the rest of the historical stuff. Without wi-fi reception, I assume it's the only way anyone in this place can communicate.

She picks up the cordless phone and says, "Yes, Spencer?"

A frown appears between her brows and she glances at me before saying, "Our new guest, Lucy Phillips, has arrived and will need to be escorted to her room."

Whatever Spencer says displeases Cora further as her lips pinch in tight disapproval. "Fine. Don't be late."

She slams the handset down and I jump, surprised by her blatant show of animosity toward an employee in front of me. As if belatedly realizing I'm here, she squares her shoulders and beams at me like that altercation I just witnessed didn't happen.

"You're in room thirteen," she says, opening a drawer and handing me a key attached to a thin piece of wood with the Viking compass logo on it. "I'll show you where it is."

Maybe she's not used to doing the menial tasks like showing guests to their rooms and that's why she's in a snit with Spencer. Whatever the reason, it's none of my business and I stand and flip the key over. On the back of the wood is another symbol as unique as the *vegvisir*. This one has what looks like a six-legged spider at the end of double lines that forms a weird cross, with a swirl and a bucket.

She notices me studying it and says, "That's another symbol from Norse mythology, a *vatnahlifir*. It's a stave that offers protection from drowning."

Considering the closeness to the beach and the swamps surrounding Arcania, I can understand the superstition, but not the sorrow in her eyes.

"My daughter drowned in the swamp close to here. Presumed to be taken by an alligator."

I'm startled by her revelation but also saddened. What must it be like to run this place, knowing your daughter died near here?

"I'm sorry to hear that."

"It happened a long time ago," she says, as we turn left at the bottom of the stairs. To my horror, tears sting my eyes and she notices. "My dear, please don't be sad. While I'll never forget the tragedy, I've come to terms with my sorrow."

"My mom died recently," I blurt, the grief gripping me at this inopportune moment precipitated by Cora's trials. "It's going to take me a long time to come to terms with anything."

"So that's why you're here," she murmurs, laying a comforting hand on my shoulder. "You've come to the right place, Lucy. We'll look after you. You'll be nurtured and cared for in your time of sorrow."

I mutter my thanks, embarrassed for revealing too much. I've come here to search for answers, not blurt the truth too soon.

"Would you like dinner sent up tonight?" She stops outside room thirteen. It's at the end of a long corridor that I've barely noticed while keeping my head down and trying not to cry. "Guests usually eat together in the dining room, but there's always the option to have room service if you prefer a quiet night in."

"That sounds good, thanks."

She holds out her hand, and I place the key in it. But the oddest thing happens; I can still feel the weight of the key's wooden fob in my hand, along with a residual heat in my palm, like I've been branded.

I flex my fingers a few times and glance at my palm, a shiver dancing across the back of my neck.

I swear the outline of the logo is imprinted on my skin, but when I blink and refocus, it's gone.

CHAPTER 6

CORA

T HEN

As HARLAN LEADS me to my room on the ground floor, I try not to ogle the opulence of my surroundings. The velvet drapes and chaise lounges, the sweeping staircase, the gilt-edged paintings of ships and formidable Vikings. I know they're Vikings because one of Mom's loser ex-boyfriends had been obsessed with historical documentaries, particularly anything to do with shipwrecks.

Seeing the direction of my gaze as we walk down a corridor off the main foyer, Harlan says, "Those are my ancestors."

"Scary dudes," I say.

"Yeah, they're responsible for all this." He sweeps his hand wide. "Got to love a good shipwreck filled with gold."

"Nice tale." I roll my eyes. "What do you think I am, a gullible ten-year-old?"

He laughs, and it transforms his face from handsome to gorgeous, and my heart races in response. "It's true. This place has tunnels underneath it that lead directly to the sea. My great-great-great-grandfather had this house built and set up the family as the sole importers of foreign delicacies in these parts."

"That's so many greats, how do I even know if it's true?"

"You're a cynical one, aren't you?" He tilts his head, studying me. "You'll just have to trust me."

"I don't trust anybody." Learned that the hard way. "But it's interesting, nonetheless."

"Many of the people who stay here grow to love it." He pins me with an enigmatic stare I have no hope of interpreting. "You'll see."

A little shiver ripples over me, like a million butterflies dancing across my skin, and I suppress the urge to shake it off.

"Here we are," he says, stopping outside a door at the end of the corridor. It's not numbered and has an ornate wrought-iron doorknob with a keyhole beneath it. "This sticks sometimes, so you'll need to jiggle it."

He rams a key in it to demonstrate, doing a half twist as he rattles the doorknob until it turns. The door creaks as it swings open and I stifle a grin. This place is really taking the gothic atmosphere to extremes.

"Hope you're comfortable here." He stands aside, allowing me to enter the room first, and I struggle not to gape.

A giant four-poster bed monopolizes the room, set high on a raised platform and draped in more of that purple velvet I'd seen in the foyer. It's covered in a black satin duvet and matching pillows, with a weird compass symbol embossed on everything.

There's an antique full-length oval mirror next to a chest of drawers, and a matching mahogany wardrobe opposite, but that monstrous bed dominates the room and I can't tear my eyes away from it.

Either Harlan doesn't see me gawking or he pretends not to notice, crossing the room to open a door. "There's a private bathroom through here. It's stocked with everything you may need. Towels are laundered twice weekly, and I can show you where all that happens later. We share meals in the dining room or outside, wherever you're more comfortable. And I'll give you the grand tour of the grounds once you're settled."

I take a tentative step into the room, feeling like I've stepped into a fairytale. But I gave up believing in those a long time ago, around the time Mom sold all my books to buy vodka when I was nine, and I can't let my guard down, no matter how amazing this is.

"You're overwhelmed," he says, approaching me cautiously, as if scared I'll bolt. "Take your time. Get settled. And come outside to meet everyone when you're ready."

I finally unglue my tongue from the roof of my mouth. "Okay, thanks."

"My room's at the other end of the corridor."

I don't know why he's telling me this, but as our gazes lock, something undefinable sizzles between us and that shivery sensation is back, making me want to rub my arms.

"I'll see you later," he says, his smile genuine, but secrets lurk in his eyes as he heads for the door.

I wait until he closes it before sinking to the floor and hugging my knees to my chest, wondering what I've gotten myself into.

CHAPTER 7
LUCY

Cora hadn't been kidding about the rooms. With the ash floorboards, slanted roofline, ecru furniture, and sleek gray bathroom, my home for the next week is ultra-modern and I love it. I've never stayed in anything so opulent.

Our brownstone in Manhattan is sparse and under-stated. Mom made it into a sanctuary and it's home to me, but this space is something I envisage myself living in once I'm a world-famous author. Ha. As if. I actually have to get words down on paper for that to happen and with a severe case of writer's block for the last few weeks, that's increasingly unlikely.

I know I'm being hard on myself because all I've done is wallow since Mom's devastating death, but I've lost the urge to write completely and can't see it returning. I'll give it time, but the spark just isn't there anymore and I wonder if I'll ever find joy in writing again.

My eyes immediately zero in on the small bookcase near the bed and I cross the room to squat and peruse the titles, an eclectic mix of genre fiction, biographies and historicals. I slide a hardcover out, OUTER BANKS TREA-SURE, intrigued by the now-familiar Viking compass on the spine. I give it a quick flick-through, knowing I'm going to read this cover to cover over the next week because I need to discover the link between the compass emblem and Mom, so I place it on the bedside table.

I'm not sure how forthcoming Cora's going to be with information. She seems friendly enough, but the way she looked at me earlier, like she knows I have an ulterior motive for coming here...it gave me the creeps.

I open the blinds and can't see much beyond a lit path leading to a pavilion I assume is the day spa. Darkness descends quickly here and I slide open the heavy glass door and step onto a small balcony, inhaling the tangy brine from an ocean I can faintly hear. The grounds are quiet and nothing like the gardens at the hotel I stayed in at Atlantic City once for a librarian conference, where guests mingled outside any time of day or night.

Without access to televisions, computers or any digital devices, I'm not sure what guests do here at night and I hope I'm not expected to join in any group activities. I have no desire to make small talk or feign interest in other people when I'm here for one reason only: to discover why my mom had that Viking emblem tattooed on the sole of her foot and how it's linked to Arcania.

I hear a soft knock at the door and head back into the room. When I open the door, I struggle not to stare at the man holding a large tray covered in two silver cloches. Not that there's anything particularly remarkable about him, but he's vaguely familiar and I'm struggling to work out how I could recognize someone here when I've never been beyond the state of New York.

The way he's staring at me, like I'm a puzzle he can't

quite figure out, makes me wonder if he's experiencing the same odd déjà vu as me.

"Excuse me, Ms. Phillips. Cora said you wanted dinner in your room tonight?"

"Yes, please, come in." I step back, slightly annoyed at Cora's presumptuousness. When she mentioned me eating in my room, I envisaged ordering something from a room service menu, not being served like a child with no choice.

"I hope this meal is suitable." He places the tray on the small circular table next to the bookcase and removes the cloches. "All guests have the same lunches and dinners, with strict dietary guidelines followed, and according to the food intolerance questionnaire you filled out online."

That explains the lack of choice. Curious, I glance at my dinner, relieved when I spy what looks like lasagna and salad, and a minuscule chocolate mousse for dessert.

"I'll get your bottled water," he says, and even his walk as he lopes toward the door is familiar.

When he re-enters the room and places two bottles beside my bed, he says, "Apologies for not introducing myself. I'm Spencer."

"Pleased to meet you," I say, and he manages a small smile along with a nod. "You've worked here a long time, Cora said."

"Yes. Over forty years."

"Wow. You must really love your job."

"Some places are hard to leave," he murmurs, his cryptic comment accompanied by a stare I have no hope of interpreting. "If there's nothing else, I'll leave you to your dinner?"

"Thanks, I'll be fine." I point at the book on my bedside table. "Though I'd love to chat to you sometime over the next week. I'm a librarian back in Manhattan and I'm slightly obsessed with all things mythological, so the history of Arcania fascinates me, especially the Viking angle."

He freezes, like I've said something inexplicably bad, but before I can ask what's wrong he gives an odd little bow and vanishes out the door like a ghost.

I shake my head and flick the lock on the door. It stands to reason a person who's been in the same job for that long in a place like this might be a tad eccentric, but there's something oddly familiar about Spencer I can't put my finger on.

Just what I need, another mystery to solve while I'm here.

CHAPTER 8
CORA

T HEN

AFTER HARLAN LEAVES THE ROOM, I slip off my shoes and socks and crawl under the covers of my princess bed. There's no other word for it, perched on a pedestal and draped in all that satin and velvet. I'm filthy and should have a shower first, but I'm bone-deep tired and can barely muster the strength to toss the throw pillows off the bed and pull back the heavy duvet before sliding under the covers.

A distinct smell of lavender warring with rose emanates from the sheets and I burrow my face into the pillow, finding the fragrance oddly comforting. I fall asleep instantly and when I next open my eyes, light is streaming through the drapes I could've sworn were closed yesterday.

I use my pinkies to remove the grit from the corners of my eyes, stretch, and roll onto my side to find a note propped on the bedside table. I stiffen and sit bolt upright.

Someone's been in my room while I slept.

My eyes dart to where I dropped my duffel yesterday and I sigh in relief when I see it hasn't moved. But that doesn't mean someone hasn't rifled it.

I slide out of bed to check and nearly fall flat on my face, forgetting the stupid raised platform the bed is perched on. Glancing at the time on a mini-grandfather clock on a dresser, I'm shocked to see it's eleven a.m., meaning I've slept for sixteen hours straight.

After a quick look through my duffel reassures me nothing has been taken, I pick up the note. The paper is cool and thick between my fingers. I unfold it, impressed by the bold cursive script.

Dear Cora,

Welcome to Arcania. We asked a staff member to leave you a breakfast tray and this note for whenever you wake.

Harlan mentioned you're seeking work, and as it happens, we have a job vacancy.

Magnus and I look forward to meeting you.

Warm regards,

Helga Medville.

While I don't appreciate some random dude entering my room while I've been sleeping, it's nice for Harlan's mom to welcome me like this. Besides, I'm starving and my stomach rumbles as my gaze sweeps the room searching for the breakfast tray. It's perched on a tiny round table in the corner that I hadn't noticed last night, a plate covered in one of those silver domes I've seen on cooking shows on TV.

There's a glass of orange juice, a tiny white jug, and a tub of yogurt arranged around the plate, and my stomach rumbles again.

I make a dash for the bathroom before whipping off that dome to find a generous wedge of vegetable quiche and a side salad. I salivate as I shovel food into my mouth, the freshness of the ingredients and the liberal use of herbs making my tastebuds dance. I have never eaten anything like this before and if this is the quality of food I can look forward to if I work here, sign me up now.

After I demolish my brunch and take a quick shower, it's almost midday and I'm embarrassed to be meeting Harlan's parents so late in the day. I'm sure they expect their workers to be tending the orchard at the crack of dawn and me sleeping in like this won't look good.

Then again, this first meeting will be as much about me sizing them up, too. I don't know these people. Their son picked me up at a roadside cafe. I'm not so gullible that I'll stay if I get a bad vibe.

But I'm also not stupid. I'm desperate for work. I need to save money to gain true independence and I expected to have to job search longer. To have one land in my lap... it's a godsend. I can't afford to screw this up because I have major trust issues.

Wearing my cleanest jeans and best top, a floating floral chiffon with a handkerchief hem in the palest of blues, I head down the corridor leading to the foyer. The place appears more welcoming in daylight, less gothic-oppressive, though those creepy Viking paintings with eyes that seem to follow me haven't changed.

As I step into the elaborate foyer, a guy appears out of nowhere and I jump, my annoyed glare fading as I get a good look at him.

If Harlan is handsome, this guy is gorgeous. He has serious bad boy vibes going on, from his dark chocolate curls, hazel eyes and stubble to his high cheekbones and square jaw. He exudes restrained energy. His eyes glow with it and as his lips ease into a lazy smile, I'm speechless.

"Sorry for spooking you," he says, his deep voice as impressive as the rest of him. "Spencer Hadley."

I remember Harlan mentioning a Spencer yesterday, the employee who runs the household. He seems awfully young to hold such a responsible position.

Spencer holds out his hand, and I stare at it like an idiot before my brain switches into gear. As our hands meet, a tiny zap shoots up my arm and I resist the urge to pull back. If he feels it too, he doesn't show it, his gaze holding mine in some weird hypnotic thing I can't look away from.

When he releases my hand, I'm cold and crave his touch again. What the hell is happening to me? I'm pragmatic, not romantic, but in the last twenty-four hours I've practically swooned over two different guys.

"You came into my room this morning," I say, brash and abrasive, folding my arms across my chest. "That's not cool."

"I know, but Helga insisted I leave you something to eat." He shrugs, like his intrusion means little. "Personally, I would've left the tray outside your door and slid the note under it, but she was adamant and as you'll soon see when you meet her, she's a hard woman to say no to."

"Maybe try harder next time," I mutter, and he laughs at my drollness.

"How did you sleep?"

I want to say 'none of your business' but if I get a job here we'll be co-workers so it's better to be polite. Besides, part of my prickliness stems from my body's irrational response to his hotness and that's not his fault.

"Good, considering I slept for sixteen hours straight."

"You must've needed it." He fixes me with a probing stare, like he's trying to see right through me. "Where are you from?"

"Miami."

I could lie but what's the point? It's not like I'll be sent back there. That's why I waited until I was eighteen to escape. From now on, I'm the boss of me.

"Nice. So what brings you to the Outer Banks?"

He's doing that weird stare thing again, and it feels like I'm bathed in a warm glow.

"Opportunity," I say, when it's blind luck.

After buying several tickets to various states and changing buses, I ended up in Nag's Head by pure chance and, thrust into the path of Harlan Medville. I'm not sure whether to be thanking fate yet, but for the first time in a long time, I slept without fear. Maybe that's why I slumbered so long? Not just exhaustion but peace, knowing some creep wouldn't be trying to enter my room.

"You've come to the right place," he says. "The Medvilles are great to work for."

"How long have you worked here?"

"Two years."

"Harlan said you manage the house. Why not work outside?"

"Because I've got a brain for figures and they liked what I did with a few wholesalers they deal with, juggling the numbers and improving their profit margins."

"I thought Harlan was the economic whiz?"

He cocks his head, studying me. "You're awfully blunt."

"Got a problem with that?"

"Nope. But people who usually arrive here are more…" He glances away, as if he's said too much.

"More what?"

When he looks back at me, I can't fathom the emotion in his eyes. "Broken," he says softly, before giving a little shake as if rousing. "Ready to meet the Medvilles, or would you prefer to look around first?"

My stomach is in knots at the thought of meeting my prospective employers, but I'd like to do it sooner rather than later so I know where I stand employment-wise, so I say, "I'd like to meet them now."

He gives a terse nod and I fall into step beside him as we follow a long, dark corridor leading off into the foyer. His silence is unnerving and I want to ask what he meant by saying most people who come here are broken, but maybe I don't need to. If anyone understands what it means to be broken, I do. My first crack appeared at around six, when Mom forgot my birthday because she had a date with a rich old dude, and those cracks continued to splinter throughout my childhood as she let me down repeatedly, until I resembled nothing more than a shattered mirror.

It makes sense that others who've possibly endured hardship and are looking for a fresh start choose to work here too: off the grid, in the fresh air, without the secrets of their past dogging their every move. I hope Arcania offers me the same reprieve.

I'm nervous about meeting Harlan's parents and when Spencer stops outside an ornate door and knocks before opening it, I wish I'd taken that tour of the place first so I know what I'm getting myself into.

When I see the couple standing by a fireplace, my nerves aren't appeased. They're giants. Helga's at least six feet and Magnus clears her by another six inches. They're big, blond, broad-shouldered, and look like they could row a Viking ship from Iceland to the United States without breaking a sweat.

Before Spencer can introduce me, Helga steps forward with her hands outstretched. "You must be Cora. Harlan's told us so much about you. It's lovely to meet you."

Thrown off guard by her unexpected effusiveness, I place my hands in hers, wishing we could've done a simple shake. She has man hands—huge—and they engulf mine in a grip that has me struggling to hold back a wince.

Magnus steps up beside his wife and thankfully holds out his hand, meaning Helga has to release mine. "Hello, Cora."

I manage a sedate "hi" as I shake his hand, confused by their constant beaming, like I'm some prodigal daughter who has returned home.

"Harlan mentioned you're looking for work?" Helga asks, gesturing to an overstuffed chair. "Why don't we sit and discuss it?"

"Okay." I glance at Spencer, who gives me a thumbs up sign of encouragement before leaving the room. Weird that the Medvilles didn't even acknowledge him. "Yes, I'm seeking employment."

"We do have a vacancy here at the moment," Magnus says. "So your arrival is rather timely."

"Have you worked before, dear?" Helga hasn't let up with the smiling and it's slightly off-putting. "What are your skills?"

"I've worked part time in a diner for a few years, so I'm great with customers. And I'm a fast learner. I'm also resourceful, dedicated and driven."

"Impressive," Helga says, while Magnus nods. "The role here is rather ambiguous, meaning you'll be picking apples in the orchards sometimes, or helping Daphne in the kitchen, or assisting Spencer with the general running of the place—"

"The position comes with a lot of responsibility," Magnus interrupts. He's lost the smile, and a frown grooves his bushy brows. "Do you think you can handle it?"

I don't tell my new employers I would've been happy cleaning toilets if it gained me steady work and a regular paycheck. "Absolutely. I'm a hard worker and I won't let you down."

"We're counting on it, dear."

I can't fathom the meaningful glance that passes between them. Maybe I don't want to? The Melville's are a tad odd and their house a little creepy, but considering what I've run from, how bad can this be?

CHAPTER 9

LUCY

I sleep surprisingly well. At home, I take ages to fall asleep and since Mom died, insomnia has plagued me. Every night I spend hours reading, often having to flick back to the previous page because I have absorbed nothing, until I finally fall asleep around three thirty in the morning. I wake unrested, with a pounding head and gritty eyes, hoping that Mom's death has been a nightmare. But in those few seconds it takes for me to struggle to consciousness I know my hope is futile and she's really gone. And another yawning day stretches before me where I wander through the apartment, too grief-stricken to pack away her things, too sad to do much else than wallow.

It must've been sheer exhaustion that helped me fall asleep last night, my first in Arcania, but I can't remember much beyond drinking my bottled water, then passing out into welcome oblivion.

After showering and dressing, I follow the corridor back to the foyer, its grandiosity striking anew. I understand wanting to preserve the history of the place, but it's so dark and gothic compared with the rooms that the contrast is startling. Three corridors branch off from the foyer, not including the one I've just traversed. The one opposite leads to more rooms, the other two have signs over them: DINING ROOM and RECREATION ROOMS.

I'm not in the mood to have breakfast with a bunch of strangers, but I'm starving, so I follow the corridor toward the dining room, not surprised there isn't a hint of bacon or pancakes in the air. While last night's dinner was yummy, I fully expect to consume my body weight in quinoa, tofu, and chia seeds at this wellness center, and I'm sure breakfast will comprise oats, granola, and fruit bowls.

The corridor is short and opens into a stunningly modern room with soaring wood-lined ceilings, pristine white walls that are unadorned, and ivory marble tiles on the floor that are so clean I could eat off them. A long ash table that seats thirty dominates the room, with a juice bar in one corner and a buffet table covered in fruit and cereals in the other. There's no one around and I head for the juice bar, pleased to see a selection of pre-made smoothies in takeout cups.

After selecting an exotic blend of papaya, lychee and pineapple, I retrace my steps, and this time choose the corridor leading to the recreation rooms. I pass a yoga studio, a Pilates room filled with intimidating equipment, a gym, and a meditation room. All are empty. The corridor ends at a heavy glass door that leads outside and that's when I spy a few hardy souls—two couples—doing yoga on a patch of grass dappled with sunlight. The serenity is inviting and I could do with a stretch, but I want to explore. I only have a week to discover how Mom is connected to this place, and I can't afford to dither.

There are orchards to my left and two paths on my right. One's a swamp walk, the other leads to the beach. After hearing how Cora's daughter drowned in the swamp, I choose the path to the beach. It's a leisurely walk through bushes that soon gives way to dunes, the soothing pounding of the ocean in the distance a welcome reprieve from my thoughts.

I'm not sure what I expect to find at Arcania, but unless I start asking questions my week will be over all too soon and I'll be back in Manhattan still wondering about Mom. But I can't barge into this. I need to be discreet and I know who to start with.

Spencer.

Last night, he'd mentioned working here for over forty years, so if Mom spent any time here, he'd know her. She had me at eighteen and I want to know what drove a young, possibly pregnant, teen away from here and why.

As if my thoughts conjure him up, Spencer appears on the path walking toward me. He's wearing a wetsuit and holding diving equipment and stops when he sees me.

"Hey." I raise my hand in greeting and he manages a stiff nod.

"Good morning. Sleep well?"

I nod. "I did. Must be the sea air."

"The tranquility is a welcome reprieve for many," he says, sounding like he's reciting a rehearsed spiel from Arcania's website and already glancing over my shoulder like he can't wait to get away.

"I bet." I point to his equipment. "At the risk of stating the obvious, you've been diving?"

"Yes. Arcania was known for it back in the day, and I can't seem to break the habit."

49

"Do guests have the opportunity to dive?"

"No." Short, sharp, curt. "It's too dangerous out there for the less experienced."

"I had a quick flip through a book in my room last night, something about Outer Banks treasure. I expect there are plenty of shipwrecks around here. Are you diving for gold?"

I expect him to smile at my flippancy. Instead, a shadow clouds his eyes and his lips thin. "Don't believe everything you hear about this place."

"I have heard little, which is why I want to ask you a few questions. As I already mentioned last night, I'm a librarian and mythology fascinates me, but I don't know much about Icelandic history and—"

"Sorry, I really have to get back," he says, a deep frown grooving his brow as he brushes past me.

But I won't be deterred. I haven't come here for the ocean air. I need someone to steer me in the right direction and what better person than a long-term employee? "You mentioned you've worked here for four decades, so I'm hoping you can help me. Did you ever know a woman named Ava Reynolds?"

He stiffens, every muscle in his back turning rigid and clearly delineated by the clinging rubber of his suit. When he glances over his shoulder, his expression is frigid, his eyes eerily blank.

"You should leave this place," he whispers, so softly I wonder if I've imagined the warning.

"Now, before it's too late," he adds, before turning and striding away like he can't get away from me fast enough.

Stunned, I take a sip of my smoothie to ease the tightness of my throat. It doesn't help and for a moment I wonder if I should heed the warning of a crazy guy who's obviously worked here too long and is caught up in some mystical beliefs.

But I can't dismiss the vision of my mom lying on that metal slab in the M.E.'s office and that tattoo on her foot.

Someone here has answers, and I'm determined to discover the truth.

CHAPTER 10
CORA

T HEN

THE MEDVILLES WEREN'T wrong when they said my role here would be ambiguous. Two weeks into my stay at Arcania and I've peeled thousands of potatoes with Daphne, I've diced onions and peppers until my fingers cramped, I've learned the difference between using cilantro and parsley for flavoring, and I've itemized every fitting in the mansion that needs replacing with Spencer.

No surprise that working with Spencer is my favorite. He's cute and charming and makes the most onerous task fun, like cleaning the frames of countless paintings. I'm not one to let my guard down, but he's so nice I look forward to seeing him every day.

Until Harlan returns.

I haven't seen him since that first night he brought me to Arcania. Spencer said he was at an organic produce conference, and his parents joined him the next day following my interview. Weird, to be employed yet not feel like I'm on a trial period being watched. Then again, I don't really know Spencer and Daphne well, so maybe they're watching me and will report back to Helga and Magnus.

It's a dreary morning and I'm taking a break, about to stroll along the boardwalk bordering the swamp with Spencer, when Harlan pulls up alongside us. I sense Spencer stiffen beside me and I can't understand the death glare Harlan shoots him.

"What are you two doing?"

When the usually garrulous Spencer doesn't answer, I say, "We're going for a walk to clear our heads of the fumes from polishing the banisters all morning."

Harlan's eyes narrow, and I'm not sure whether my answer or the fact I'm taking a walk with Spencer displeases him. He almost appears jealous, which is crazy, considering we barely know each other.

Sensing Harlan's displeasure, Spencer says, "I'll see if Daphne needs a hand," before scuttling away.

I'm so shocked by the change in the cocky guy I've got to know over the last two weeks that I stare after him until Harlan clears his throat.

"Don't waste your time crushing on him. He toys with all the new girls."

Stunned by his presumptuousness, I'm about to tell him where he can stick his unsolicited advice, when he grimaces and flashes me a sheepish smile. "Sorry. I'm not good with... uh... girls I like."

Shock number two in as many minutes. Why would a guy who's a virtual stranger confess to liking me?

When I say nothing, he shakes his head, kills the engine, and gets out of his car. He's wearing navy chinos, a white polo, and a designer sports jacket that looks tailor made. It's crazy that a guy who can't be much older than me is so well put together while can barely snag my hair in a ponytail and splash water on my face most mornings.

He screws up his nose. "I've made a real mess of this, haven't I?"

The intensity of his stare disarms me and I blurt, "I'm confused."

He takes a step closer, and I get a flashback to the night he brought me here, when his proximity gave me the shivers—in a good way. "I know this is crazy because we hardly know each other, but I felt a connection when we first met and I want to explore that."

He doesn't break eye contact and he sounds genuine, but for all I know, he does this with all the new girls, just as he's accused Spencer of doing.

"What do you mean?"

"Go out with me."

"On a date?" I make a scoffing sound that comes out an embarrassing snort. "Yeah, like your parents will be impressed with the hired help dating their mega-rich son."

"My parents like you."

"After interviewing me for five seconds?" I roll my eyes. "Look, I enjoy working here and I'm grateful you brought me to Arcania, but I'm not that desperate for work that you think you can mess with me."

His frown reappears. "It's not like that."

"Really? Because from where I'm standing, it's exactly like that."

A tiny vein pulses near his right temple, but his posture remains relaxed, like he's sure I'll give in eventually. I don't like smugness. "Give me a chance."

"To do what?"

He opens his mouth to respond, before closing it again and looking over my shoulder at the swamp. An awkward silence stretches between us and I'm on the verge of turning away and starting my walk, when he says, "I need you to trust me."

I don't trust anyone, least of all some rich dude who picked me up at a roadside cafe and appears too good to be true.

But I give a wary nod and for now it's enough as his eyes lose the anguish, like he's been hanging on my answer.

"Have you had a chance to see the orchards yet?"

I'm grateful for his abrupt change of subject because the thought of the two of us dating is incongruous and I can't afford to do anything to jeopardize this job. Whatever Harlan may say, I'm pretty sure Magnus and Helga will boot me out of here if they think I'm interested in their son.

"Not really. I've walked past the orchards but haven't explored fully. Daphne and Spencer have kept me busy working inside the last few weeks."

I find it odd I haven't had time to venture outside much, let alone meet anyone else. I'm the only worker living in the house at the moment. The rest, couples mostly, are inhabiting the tents. I barely see them. They're up earlier than me and already in the orchards by the time I'm in the kitchen helping prep their lunch and dinner, and I can't see their tents from my bedroom window.

I'd mentioned introducing myself to them to Spencer once, but he'd been oddly recalcitrant, saying they kept to themselves and didn't treat us—the employees who worked in the house—the same, seeing us as outsiders. I'd rather not risk having anyone against me while I'm trying to make a good impression in my first few weeks here, so I'd steered clear.

"If you're keen to take a walk, why don't you skip the boardwalk and I'll show you around the orchards?"

I'd rather be alone, but that fervent glint in his eyes is back and I don't want to appear churlish. Besides, spending more time with this enigmatic guy can't be a bad thing. I can't get a proper read on him and I want to.

Starting now.

CHAPTER 11

LUCY

After a long walk on the beach to shake off Spencer's bizarre warning and an hour of reading in my room, I meet my fellow guests at lunch. Craig and Demi are a delightful couple who finish each other's sentences and are here because it's the one week a year they take off from their thriving social influencer career across all platforms. Jase and Cindy are practically newlyweds who barely hear a word the rest of us say, they're that in love. They work in IT and want a second honeymoon after a heinous job that involved reconfiguring the data systems for a hospital in Florida that ransomware had corrupted.

I can't deny I'm fascinated by my fellow digi-detoxers, mainly because they take my mind off brooding about Mom, and I make small talk over a delicious lunch of vegetable burritos and fruit salad. No staff are in sight and we help ourselves from the monstrous platters laid on the table.

"Does anyone actually work here?" Craig asks, gesturing at the empty dining room. "Our friends who've been coming here the last few years warned us about the isolation and implied that the place appears deserted most of the time, even with other guests around."

Demi snickers. "Craig's best friend spooks easily and swears this place is haunted, which is why no staff stick around, and now that we're here, Craig agrees."

I laugh too, but it's a tad uneasy, while Jase and Cindy continue to stare into each other's eyes, oblivious to our conversation. "Why do you say that?"

Craig glances over his shoulder, then leans forward a tad as if about to impart a great secret. "Don't you feel we're being watched?"

Demi rolls her eyes, but I cast a quick glance around the sparse room, looking for the possibility of hidden cameras. She laughs. "Stop it, Craig. You're scaring Lucy."

Craig tilts his nose in the air, mock offended. "Some of us have a sixth sense about stuff like this. You get it, don't you, Luce?"

I hate when people abbreviate my name, especially when they don't know me. Mom was the only one who called me Luce and, to my embarrassment, tears fill my eyes.

"See what you've done?" Demi hisses and nudges Craig, whose expression is sheepish, before she slides into the chair next to me and slings an arm over my shoulder. "Are you okay?"

I press my lips together to stifle a sob and nod, dragging in a few deep breaths, before feeling confident enough to speak without bawling. "It's nothing to do with you. My mom died recently and I'm still coming to terms with it, so the slightest thing sets me off."

"Aww, honey, I'm sorry." Demi hugs me and I see Craig mouth, "I'm sorry too," over her shoulder.

My embarrassing behavior has caught the attention of

Jase and Cindy, and they offer their murmured condolences too.

I dab at my eyes and force a smile. "Sorry, guys. I didn't mean to be a downer."

"Hey, you're not, and if you want to talk any time, I'm here," Demi says, her offer unexpected and sweet.

I'm an introvert with few friends, so it's always a surprise when a person I barely know reaches out. It's happened a few times at the library—Gerry, an old man who asked me out for coffee once after I'd helped him research his family tree online, and Beryl, an octogenarian who shared my love of paranormal novels, who'd invited me to her home for dinner. I hadn't accepted either of those invitations, but it had been nice to be asked.

"Thanks, but I'm okay." I stab a piece of watermelon with my fork and bring it to my lips when Craig says, "Perhaps you should chat with Cora? She's good at counseling, or so some of our older friends who were here years ago have said. Apparently, they worked the orchards for a while before moving on."

I have no intention of unburdening myself to Cora but if Craig and Demi have friends who were around back then, maybe they knew my mom?

"How long ago was that?"

Craig screws up his face, thinking. "About twenty-six years ago. I remember it because it's the year she lost her daughter to that alligator attack in the swamp."

Demi shudders. "We avoid that boardwalk no matter how safe it supposedly is now."

I'm twenty-five, so my mom could've been around back then. Maybe she wanted some time out before she got pregnant or had me? It will be a bonus if Craig's friends worked here at the same time as my mom. "Do you think your friends would mind if I reached out to them once I leave here? I'm a sucker for history, and my librarian curiosity is piqued by this place."

"I'll ask, but I'm sure they'll be fine with it," Craig says. "Though Cora would be an excellent source of knowledge on Arcania's history."

"Just don't mention Ava and you'll be fine," Demi adds, oblivious to my stiffening beside her as a trickle of something otherworldly tiptoes down my spine.

Demi pronounced it Ay-va when Mom's name, despite being spelled Ava, was sounded out as Ar-va, yet I'm still freaked. I don't believe in coincidences. I'm too practical for that.

"Who's Ava?" I ask, suspecting the answer before either of them respond.

"Cora's daughter that died," Craig says. "Apparently Cora goes crazy if you mention her."

I manage to say, "I won't," while my mind reels from the implications of this.

What are the odds of my mom and Cora's daughter sharing a name, both connected to this place?

Now, more than ever, I need to understand my mom's link to Arcania.

CHAPTER 12

CORA

T HEN

THE ORCHARDS ARE ODDLY DESERTED as Harlan gives me the grand tour. I see a few workers taking a lunch break in the distance, sitting on wrought-iron benches, their faces tilted to the sun like they don't have a care in the world.

What I wouldn't give to feel like that.

My fear of being pawed—or worse—by one of Mom's boyfriends may have abated, but I'm still worried that I can lose this job at any moment and I'll be back at square one, homeless and jobless. I've never felt carefree but I hope with some hard work and careful saving, I'll be able to support myself and have some extra for when I need it.

"We're the largest producer of organic fruit and vegetables in all of North Carolina," Harlan says, gesturing to the trees and neat rows of plants around us. "Tomatoes, sweet bell peppers, radishes, zucchini, eggplant, beets, turnips, squash, watermelon, and sweet potatoes. You name it, we supply it."

"Impressive," I say, not really caring about the local produce and more interested in discovering why this wealthy, worldly guy likes me.

I'm not an idiot. I'm pretty enough—blonde hair, blue eyes, straight teeth, decent body—but someone like Harlan could have his pick of women. And considering how rich he is, I'm pretty sure Helga and Magnus would have him earmarked to marry an equally wealthy socialite in the area.

Which leaves my first assumption—he thinks he can toy with the hired help, then discard me—as being the most accurate. But I can't ignore the frisson of excitement that zaps me whenever our hands accidentally brush as we walk. It's the first time I've been remotely attracted to a guy like him, and it's heady stuff for a girl like me.

"But that's not the only thing we're famous for." He touches me on the arm, the briefest brush of his fingertips, and I feel the sizzle all the way to my toes. "Remember when I mentioned the shipwreck not far off the coast here and the treasure?"

"Yeah, and I already told you I'm too old for fairytales."

His smile makes my stomach flip. "There are a lot of myths that surround Arcania, but the sunken treasure is real. There's a gold compass engraved with our emblem, the *vegvisir*, that is priceless. Collectors from all around the world would kill to get their hands on it."

I don't care about some lost artifact, but Harlan's eyes are glowing with fervor and he's gorgeous when he's passionate.

"Tell me more. Like what's a *vegvisir*, for example."

"It's a Viking compass. You would've seen it on the

bedding and linen in your room. Embossed into the soap. On everything. It's the symbol of finding your way and supposedly has magical powers. My forefathers revered it enough to ensure everything here is tied to it."

He hesitates and oddly, he's staring at the ground, his foot, more precisely.

"What's wrong?"

His gaze sweeps my face like he's searching for answers, and before I can call him on his strange behavior, he rests a hand on my shoulder and removes his shoe and sock with the other.

"Sorry for leaning on you. My balance is hopeless," he says, raising his bare foot so I can see the sole, where the emblem he's been raving about is tattooed in turquoise ink on his heel. "I meant it when I said everything in Arcania is bound by this symbol."

I wince. "Did that hurt? I know the sole is one of the toughest parts of the body, but surely it's sensitive too?"

"It was worth it." He lowers his foot and removes his hand from my shoulder. Bizarrely, I miss the contact. "Everyone who wants to be part of Arcania and potentially share in its wealth gets one."

I know what's coming before he opens his mouth and I want to yell 'no way no how' am I getting a tattoo. I have no idea how long I'll stay here; probably a few more weeks to add to my savings. Then again, where else am I going to find a rent-free place to stay while getting paid to work? Not to mention the incredible healthy meals courtesy of the organic produce.

But a tattoo? Do I look like a cow who wants to be branded?

"Share in its wealth? Sounds like you're trying to promote a pyramid scheme."

He laughs. "You really are a cynic, aren't you?"

"I'm a realist. There's a difference."

"Well, Miss Realist, I have a feeling I won't need to convince you of anything after you spend some time with us." He sits to put on his sock and shoe and pats the ground next to him. "You don't know me and by your expression earlier when I said the same thing, you probably think this is a line, but I definitely felt that we had a connection the moment we met."

A faint blush stains his cheeks. It's adorable. "My mom always said I'd know when I met 'the one' and at the risk of scaring you off, I think that's you, Cora."

Warmth surges into my face, but I try to play it cool. I've never had anyone look at me the way Harlan is at the moment: like he can see all the way down to my tender bruised soul and wants to make me whole.

I'm so off balance by his intense attention I resort to flippancy. "You're right. I think it's a line."

He reaches up and trails a fingertip along my jaw, setting my body alight. "All I ask is that you have a little faith and let me prove to you how good we can be together."

His gaze locks on mine, hypnotizing, mesmerizing, imploring me to believe him. I want to, but I wasn't lying when I told him I'm a realist. Stuff like this doesn't happen to me. Rich guy who can have anything he wants, poor girl down on her luck, that's the facts. I'll be better off remembering I'm here to save money, not fall for a glib sweet talker.

When I don't respond, he leaps to his feet and holds out his hand. "Come on, I'll show you the beach. Do you dive?"

I accept his hand and stand, not surprised when he tightens his grip. "No. I'm petrified of water."

"Too bad." He winks. "I would give anything to see you in a bikini."

I groan and yank my hand out of his so I can swat him. "You did not just say that."

He laughs so loudly a nearby bird hidden in a tree's foliage gives a loud squawk. "Lame. I know. Forgive me."

I roll my eyes, but we're grinning at each other and I'm surprisingly at ease with this guy I barely know.

"I could teach you to dive?" He holds up his hands like he has nothing to hide. "I'll be gentle, honest."

"Thanks, but I'll give the ocean a miss."

My shudder is real. One of Mom's boyfriends had thrown me in the pool when I was five and I'd swallowed enough water I thought I'd drowned. I've been terrified of being out of my depth ever since.

"That's okay. We have enough divers here searching the wreckage."

"So you actually believe all that sunken treasure stuff?"

He nods, somber. "All the workers here learn to dive if they don't know how and they take it in turns to search the wreck a few times a week."

Intrigued by an economics major who appears to believe in a myth, I ask, "Has anything been found?"

He nods. "Gold coins, mostly. Jewelry. That kind of thing."

"And here I thought you made your fortune in organic produce."

"That's our staple, but what we've salvaged from the wreck has provided a nice boost in income. Not that we've sold most of it, but the gold has come in handy during lean years."

I've had plenty of those lean years too. My small savings working part-time at the diner barely covered the necessities. I learned early on not to count on Mom for clothes and shoes, so with a little frugality and a lot of scouring second-hand shops, I got by.

What would it be like to have access to a fortune supplemented by the occasional treasure find? Definitely sounds like something out of a fairytale and if Harlan's to be believed, maybe I can be a part of it?

—

CHAPTER 13

LUCY

Now I understand why Spencer appeared so freaked out this morning when I asked him if he knew an Ava Reynolds. Hearing the first name of Cora's dead daughter even if pronounced differently must've rattled him and he didn't want to talk about it—especially if what Craig has said is true and Cora doesn't like it—so he'd scurried off.

Interestingly, if Cora doesn't like discussing her daughter's death, why did she mention it to me when I first arrived? Then again, considering I'd told her about Mom dying recently, it was probably her attempt at empathizing, trying to make a guest comfortable.

Whatever her rationale, I can't interrogate her just yet, not after what Craig said, which leaves one other person who can definitely give me answers. However, Spencer is nowhere to be found. I scour the grounds, the day spa—which is stunningly beautiful in its simplicity, all muted lights and taupe walls and lavender-scented air—before exploring the mansion from top to bottom.

Once again, I don't cross paths with anyone, and my

skin prickles with awareness as I realize how damn lonely it is in this place. There's a difference between providing a quiet environment for guests to detox and being surrounded by perpetual silence in isolation. It's a tad spooky and I don't scare easy. But I can't shake the feeling I'm being watched as I comb the grounds—nothing to do with Craig saying it, more like a feeling I can't ignore—and when I set foot inside the mansion again, my skin prickles like a million ants are on the march.

I rub my arms, unwilling to give up my search but needing to regroup and think, so I head to my room. I reach for the doorknob when I hear it, the muffled boom of a steel door closing beneath my feet.

The tunnels.

Nobody else has mentioned them apart from Spencer and I'm sure they're not part of the guest package, but who's going to see me if I snoop around? It's not like I have anything better to do. Jase and Cindy retired to their room after lunch, and Craig and Demi went on a long beach walk. The day spa is closed so I'm not sure if it's only staffed on a part-time basis, and Daphne, Spencer and Cora are the only other employees I've seen here, apart from the yoga instructor briefly this morning.

Glancing over my shoulder to ensure the corridor is deserted, I open the door opposite my room, marked 'Staff Only'. I thought it was a linen closet and expect it to be locked, but the door swings open soundlessly, a sensor light clicks on, and I release a sigh of relief when I spy regular cleaning supplies—mop, vacuum, buckets, chemicals—stacked neatly along the walls. I wasn't sure what I was expecting to find, but in this weird place anything's possible.

There's a sheet hanging on the opposite wall, covering

something, and I close the door before taking a few steps across the small closet and tugging it aside to reveal a door. Not just any door. It's huge, made of thick old planks, with a huge knob the size of a dinner plate in the middle. The knob's engraved with the *vegvisir* and is made from heavy iron with symmetrical spokes fanning out from its center like a ship's steering wheel.

I reach out to grab the spokes, surprised to find them slightly warm rather than the cold of iron I expected. Has someone recently entered or exited the tunnel? Probably staff and if so, I shouldn't be caught snooping like this.

But I came here to find answers and I won't get them by wasting my time with yoga and pilates.

Mind made up, I turn the wheel counterclockwise. It's resistant to movement and creaks, but I persist, throwing my weight behind it until I hear a satisfying clunk of bolts sliding back. The door swings open, I take a step forward, and a blast of air so cold my teeth chatter hits me like a wet blanket to the face.

I gasp, the frigid air making my legs tremble, and I reach for the walls to steady myself. My palms encounter icy slime and I yelp, snatching my hands away. I swipe them down the side of my jeans, but it doesn't stop the strange prickling, and when I glance at my palms, I see the faintest fluorescent glow of Arcania's emblem emblazoned on my skin.

I blink several times and refocus, seeing nothing but my bare palms, and I wonder if my obsession with the *vegvisir* and what it was doing tattooed on my mom's sole is making me go a little loopy.

Dragging a few deep breaths into my lungs, I wait for my eyes to grow accustomed to the gloom. The tunnel isn't pitch black. Instead, a weird glow emanates as far as I can see, the same dim lighting recreated by the library staff on Halloween by placing paper lanterns over the lights.

The cold that blasted me when I first opened the door has subsided, but I wrap my arms around my middle, regardless. I have two choices: explore this tunnel and where it leads or listen to my voice of reason, that's insisting I stop this madness and go back to my room.

I'm leaning toward the latter, but if Mom had the remotest connection to this place, I need to discover how, so I shake out my arms, square my shoulders, and take a step forward. Another. Forcing my feet to move forward when every self-preservation instinct is urging me to turn back.

The faintest tang of rotting seaweed fills my nose the deeper I move into the tunnel, darkness all around me. But it's not intensifying. If anything, the light increases with each step I take, the damp stone walls shimmering with a faint glow. I never liked chemistry in school, so don't know what's coating the stone to make it look like that and after my earlier encounter when I touched them, I don't want to find out.

The tunnel ends abruptly, opening out into a large cave where I can stand upright without hitting my head. The walls glow like the tunnel but I can't see any source of light and there's another heavy door, made of steel this time, a few feet in front of me, with the same Viking compass embossed on the steering wheel knob, and a porthole-like window set three quarters of the way up.

I'm tempted to open the door, but I barely take a step forward when a loud boom from the other side of it makes me jump.

A horrible thought insinuates its way into my brain. Is someone trapped in there?

The boom comes again, and again, and again, moments apart, and I stand, immobile, torn, wondering what to do.

That's when I hear it.

The faintest strain of *'Lucy, are you there?'*

I stifle a scream and run.

CHAPTER 14
CORA

T HEN

FOR THE NEXT WEEK, I work in the orchard during the day and spend every evening with Harlan, usually in a cove on the beach. My co-workers are an odd bunch. They're all couples and they stick together, walking around with weird smiles on their faces and talking in hushed tones. I suspect many of them are high, so I stay clear. I need my wits about me, not to be coerced into smoking or ingesting weed with a bunch of hippies.

They're amenable enough, but whenever Magnus appears, the atmosphere changes. They become subservient underlings, bowing down to a cult leader. Not literally, but that's the general impression I get, that they see him as some kind of god and will do anything to appease him.

I asked Spencer about it and he warned me not to delve

because I may not like what I find, so I mainly keep to myself when working and don't engage with the others beyond a polite nod and greeting.

As for the time spent with Harlan in a secluded cove in the evenings... I hate to admit it, but I'm falling for him against my better judgement. I can't help it. He's charming and sweet, with a bad boy edge. I can't put my finger on it, but he gives off a dangerous vibe, like anyone who gets too close will be swept up in his sphere. He's magnetic, one of those people you want to be near and are powerless to resist yet know that maybe you shouldn't get too close.

We talk about anything and everything while sheltered by that cove, sitting on a picnic blanket on the sand, sharing sandwiches and soda packed by Daphne. She's never asked Harlan why he asks for a portable supper almost every evening. Then again, she wouldn't question the boss. And if she suspects he's sharing his picnic with me, she's never said. I guess she values her job as much as I do.

When I first arrived here, I hoped Daphne and I could become friends. She's twenty, only a few years older than me, but she makes my introversion seem like I'm a party animal. Yeah, she's that quiet. She only speaks when needed—usually to order me around—but our silences are companionable as we work side by side and I'm okay with that. Better a friendly introvert than a mean co-worker.

During our evenings in the cove, Harlan talks about his plans for Arcania once he's in control—apparently his parents have hinted relinquishing the management to him within the next few years—his fervent belief the priceless gold compass exists, and his dreams for us.

The latter scares me the most, as I'm terrified of giving my heart to a guy, only to have him squash it like a bug. I've seen it happen to Mom repeatedly over the years and I vowed never to be like her, yet here I am in danger of falling for Harlan.

To offset my ridiculously spiraling crush on a guy way out of my league, I spend time with Spencer, too. He's the opposite of Harlan and he grounds me. Spencer is light to Harlan's dark, fun to his intensity, teasing to his serious- ness. I shouldn't compare the two but I can't help it. And while I'd never want to annoy Harlan, considering he's technically my employer—and has made it more than clear he sees a future for us—I know deep down if it came to a choice between the two men, I'd choose Spencer.

I'm not cut out to be a lady of the manor, which is clearly the role Harlan sees me falling into. I'll never be as polished as him, as wrapped up in Arcania, as he is. And he can reiterate repeatedly how much his parents love me, but I don't believe it. The few times we interact, Magnus and Helga are polite but distant, at complete odds with their weird effusiveness when they first hired me.

An hour ago, Harlan professed his love for me while strolling along the beach and I'd silently freaked. If he noticed I didn't say it back, he ignored it; instead, he'd demonstrated his feelings by kissing me until I was dizzy. But I'd been relieved when he had to attend a business meeting with his parents, saving me from falsely professing my feelings.

Do I like Harlan? Yes.

Do I love him? No.

Do I see a future with him? Maybe.

But it's way too early to be making declarations and after he leaves me on the beach, I continue to walk until dusk falls. The crashing waves drown out my thoughts and the briny tang of the ocean clears my head, so when I get back to Arcania I'm thinking more clearly.

If Harlan pressures me, I'll tell him I care about him, but I want to take things slow. I might even give him a snippet about my past and Mom's dramas so he understands where I'm coming from. It's not a refusal, but a clear message to slow things down.

My legs are aching from walking so far as I trudge up the path from the beach toward the house. As I near the orchard, I hear the loud boom of bass, a strange pounding rhythm that reverberates through me, and bursts of raucous laughter.

The workers are having a party, the first since I've been here. I'm tired and want to head to my room, but it'll be a good opportunity to get to know them better. I don't enjoy being the odd person out here. Not that I plan on divulging anything personal, not even to Harlan, but I'll feel better if I have a friend here, someone I can count on.

As if my wish makes him materialize, Spencer appears from between the nearest apple trees. His face lights up when he spots me and my heart gives an answering thump. It would be so easy to fall into a relationship with him but I don't want to anger Harlan. I've lucked into a steady job, I'm saving money, and I'm free. I'd be a fool to mess with that.

"Hey, Cora." He raises his hand as he lopes toward me, his strides long and easy. Everything about him is relaxed. "How was your day?"

"Good. Busy. Just getting back from a walk along the beach."

"Alone?" He wiggles his eyebrows suggestively and I laugh. "That's a shame. You can ask me to accompany you next time."

"Who says I was alone?"

He's crestfallen for a moment before his mouth eases into a grin. "Well, I know for a fact you weren't with Harlan because he's playing the dutiful son for the monthly 'going over the accounts with Mommy and Daddy.' So that leaves the door wide open for me."

I roll my eyes. "To do what?"

"Whisk you away to a party. Come on."

He holds his hand out and I stare at it for a second before quelling my inner voice, the one that's warning me I'm playing with fire by crushing on two guys and slip my hand into his.

He tugs on my hand, and I stumble against him. He chuckles and lowers his head to murmur in my ear, "That's my girl. Let's go have some fun."

I refrain from saying 'I can't be your girl' because, technically, Harlan thinks I'm his. That's when it hits me; what I'm doing, by inadvertently encouraging Spencer, could cost him—and me—our jobs.

I try to yank my hand free, but Spencer tightens his grip and then we're in the midst of the party. Everyone is dancing, whirling around and around with their arms flung overhead, the bass so loud I feel the pounding in my skull. A few people wave at me, but most appear trance-like, and I know drugs must feature in their after-hour activities too.

"You thirsty?" Spencer mouths and I nod, so we head for a trestle table covered in chips, dips and cheeses, with a giant punchbowl in the center.

"Try this. You'll like it." He scoops the punch with a ladle and pours it into a plastic cup, before handing it to me. "Daphne makes a killer tropical punch."

I take a sip and the combination of pineapple, peach, strawberries and lemonade fizz on my tongue in a delicious combination. "Mmm, good," I say, draining half the cup before Spencer says, "Whoa, go easy, tiger. That's got vodka in it too."

In response, I drink the rest in two gulps, and he laughs. "Someone's lightening up tonight."

I'm not sure if it's the vodka, the balmy night, the hypnotic music, or the look in Spencer's eyes, but I thrust my cup at him for a refill and say, "It's about time I cut loose, don't you think?"

His eyebrows rise in surprise but this time he fills a cup for himself too and we touch cups before downing our punch fast. The buzz is immediate. My head is slightly fuzzy and I'm pleasantly warm all over. And for the first time in a long time, I feel carefree.

"Want to dance?" I ask, not waiting for Spencer's response.

He's grinning at me as I slide my arms around his waist and pull him close, and then we're swaying to the music. I like this new song. It's slow. Sensual. And the heat from Spencer's body is making me burn from the inside out.

I have no idea how long we dance, our bodies pressing against each other. I lose track of time. I lose all common sense. I lose my mind as my hands slide from his waist to his butt, leaving him in little doubt about how I want tonight to end.

I want Spencer to be my first.

He eases away to look me in the eye. "Are you sure this is what you want?"

I've never been surer of anything. I've spent my entire life looking over my shoulder, being fearful of someone, trying to blend into the background. Tonight, with a sea breeze in my hair and my body languid and throbbing with need, I want to do something impulsive. Something to make me feel good. Something exciting and wondrous.

"I'm sure," I murmur, pressing a brief kiss to his lips, a promise of more.

Spencer doesn't hesitate. He takes my hand and we head deeper into the orchard. Away from everyone. Where the scent of fresh apples lingers in the air as we lose ourselves in each other.

CHAPTER 15

LUCY

The tunnel has a steeper incline on the way back, and I'm gasping for air by the time I make it back to the entrance.

To find Spencer barring my way out.

"What are you doing down here?" A deep frown slashes his brow, and he's glaring at me like he could easily lock me down here and throw away the key. "It's not safe."

Fear tightens my throat. I'm alone with a man who's already warned me I should leave Arcania in a 'Staff Only' cleaning closet, which hides an ancient tunnel leading to a freaky chamber. And considering how empty Arcania is, even if I screamed, the odds are nobody would hear me.

Sensing my distress, Spencer stands aside to let me pass. "Come out of there."

"Gladly," I mutter, stepping past him, eyeing the closet door, but wanting to interrogate him too. I'd been looking for him earlier and this seems like the perfect opportunity, despite our less than stellar surroundings.

He closes the door and swings the wheel-handle clockwise until the bolts clunk back into place. Only then does he turn toward me and thankfully, he's lost the glower.

"Was that you I heard calling out to me while I was down there?" I ask. I don't believe in ghosts but I really want him to confirm I'm not going crazy and hearing things that aren't there.

He nods, and I exhale in relief. "Yes. I saw you exploring the grounds earlier and everyone else is accounted for."

I bristle. "What do you mean, 'accounted for?' Are you spying on the guests?"

He barks out a laugh. "Nothing so nefarious. When they're only five of you here, it's pretty easy to keep tabs."

His answer doesn't assuage my concern that we're being watched, and it explains that weird feeling I'd had earlier when walking the grounds.

"Actually, I was looking for you."

His lips thin in disapproval. "Why?"

"Because I wanted to ask why you told me I should leave earlier."

He stares at me, his intense scrutiny disconcerting as the awkward silence between us grows. I'm about to give up when he says, "Arcania bears witness to many secrets, and it doesn't abide interference from outsiders."

I want to laugh off his suggestion that the house can influence its inhabitants, but his somber expression stops me.

He's not kidding.

"What are you saying?"

"That you should leave well enough alone."

Exasperated by his ominous warnings, I shake my head. "I'm not here to cause trouble."

"Then why are you here?" He points to the door leading

to the tunnel. "Because most guests who come here to digitally detox don't snoop around, especially in the tunnels."

"There's more than one?"

His sigh is almost inaudible. "Yes, but the rest are much deeper subterranean and very few are accessible from the inside of the house."

My curiosity must show on my face because he tsks-tsks. "You won't be able to find them, which is good, as they are not to be entered."

"Quit trying to scare me off."

I expect him to refute my accusation, but he remains tight-lipped, so I ask, "What's beyond that chamber down there?"

The light inside the closet isn't great, but I see Spencer pale.

After an eternity, he whispers, "You don't want to know."

He's wrong. I need answers, and his whole mysterious act is wearing thin.

"Spencer, as I said before, I'm not here to cause trouble. But I'm here to find answers to an issue I can't tell you about and I won't give up, so you can either help me or—"

"You're just like your mother," he mutters, a second before he barges through the closet door and into the corridor, leaving me stunned.

CHAPTER 16
CORA

T HEN

I'M GLOVED to my elbows, scrubbing the window frames on the east wing of the house, when Harlan taps me on the shoulder.

"I need to talk to you about something important."

I'm annoyed at being interrupted. Daphne said I only have an hour to complete this task before she needs my help in the kitchen. Then again, a lot has been annoying me lately. My mood swings over the last few weeks have been erratic. I know why. Ever since I lost my virginity to Spencer, I've been on edge; fearful Harlan will find out, regretful I led Spencer on, terrified I'll lose my job.

That punch I'd drunk at the employees' party had been potent because I never throw caution to the wind like that and once I'd sobered up the next morning, despite Spencer's reassurances he wouldn't tell anyone about our dalliance and his agreement to keep things casual, I couldn't shake the feeling I'm on the edge of imploding.

"Sounds ominous," I say, dumping the brush I'm using to scrub the sills in the bucket of suds at my feet and peeling off the gloves. "What's up?"

He glances over his shoulder, and his expression is almost fearful. "Not here," he murmurs, pointing toward the swamp. "Let's talk there so no one can overhear."

As I've learned over the last few weeks, Harlan is prone to theatrics. Not in a flamboyant way, but if there's a fuss to be made, he'll make it. I've seen him berate a worker for not inspecting the squash close enough before packing, I've seen him make a fuss over a crate of spoiled beets, and I've seen him slam the door on his parents after a confrontation he wouldn't elaborate on.

It's not in my nature to placate, especially some rich guy prone to tantrums, but for all his faults, he can be kind too. He surprised me with a picnic on the beach one night, he's encouraged me to open up during our discussions at the cove, and he's taught me a lot about the history of Arcania. I know he wants to take our relationship to the next level, but I'm not sure I want to. Then again, if my suspicions are correct, I may not have a choice in the matter.

I'm late.

And if the unthinkable has happened and I'm pregnant, I know what I have to do.

I don't want my child to have the hard life I did, being raised by a struggling single mom with limited resources. If Harlan really sees a future for us, I'd be a fool to pass it up, even if I don't love him.

It's duplicitous, sleeping with him so I won't have to reveal the truth of my baby's paternity, but I want my baby to never struggle and that's exactly what will happen if I choose Spencer. We'll be kicked out, desperately trying to find new jobs and a new place to stay, with a baby to provide for. I can't bear thinking about it. Better for Spencer to never know and for Harlan to never question.

The boardwalk flanking the swamp is wide, with room for at least four people to walk side by side, but I still avoid this area. Daphne had freaked me out the first week I'd been here with tales of alligators lurking in the murky depths just waiting for a snack and I'd steered clear ever since.

When we're in the middle of the boardwalk, far enough from the house that we can see both ways if anyone's approaching, Harlan shoots me a look I have no hope of interpreting. It's part hopeful, part manic, and it worries me. Surely he hasn't found out about Spencer and me and wants to shove me into the swamp?

"I'm going to confide in you, Cora, and I need you to promise me you won't tell anyone."

He's piqued my interest, and I hold up my hand. "Promise."

"I overhead my parents fifteen minutes ago. They were talking in the office and hadn't closed the door completely. I was going to shut it when I heard my name mentioned..." he trails off, his expression pained. "They've always led me to believe that if anything happened to them, I'd inherit Arcania. In fact, they've hinted frequently that they're ready to retire and I'm perfectly poised to take over." His lips thin. "So imagine my surprise when I heard them say a distant cousin in Iceland will inherit Arcania if anything happens to them within the next few years because I'm too young and I'm single."

He falls silent and I'm compelled to add, "That must've been tough on you hearing that."

"It gutted me." He makes a fist and jabs himself in the stomach, his vehemence startling. "But I'm not accepting it. I'll make sure I inherit Arcania, and that means I need your help."

The last thing I want is to antagonize Magnus and Helga, but Harlan needs placating. He's wild-eyed and tense, his teeth gritting so hard his jaw juts. "Not sure what I can do, but if you think I can help somehow, just let me know."

"I was hoping you'd say that." His grin is sly, and it raises my hackles a little. "If me being single and deemed irresponsible is a problem, I can rectify that. Apparently, this cousin of mine is married with a family and my parents value that stability." He waves his hand between us. "So that's what we'll give them. A marriage."

His shock announcement makes the pit of my stomach fall away, and I gape as he continues. "I know this seems crazy to you, us getting married when we haven't known each other long. But I love you, Cora. I've known from the beginning you'd make a perfect mistress of Arcania because you feel an attachment to this place as much as I do. And while it seems like I'm presenting a business proposal to you, think of the future we can have. We'll be happy and Arcania will thrive. Doesn't that sound appealing?"

I search Harlan's face for some sign he's joking; that this is an elaborate hoax he's perpetuating for the fun of it. But he's perfectly serious and I struggle to subdue a hysterical giggle.

Married at eighteen to a guy I like but don't love is so far from what I want for my life it's ludicrous.

But then I remember my unborn child and the secure future Harlan is offering us, and I'm not so dismissive.

Can I do this? Marry a virtual stranger for the sake of my child?

"Cora, say something." He takes hold of my hands, infusing me with warmth. I must be in shock because my fingers are icy. "Please, say yes. I promise I'll make you happy and we can build on the relationship we've started."

I want to say no.

I want to yank my hands free from his and run as far from this place as possible.

Instead, I force a smile and nod.

CHAPTER 17

LUCY

By the time I absorb the implication that Spencer knew my mother and reassemble my wits to go after him, he's vanished. I jog down the length of the corridor, but the foyer's empty and he's nowhere in sight.

Stunned by his revelation, I wander back to my room in a daze and flop on the bed, unsure whether to be annoyed that he didn't tell me he knew Mom when I questioned him earlier today near the beach, or elated that I'm finally getting somewhere.

Spencer knew Mom.

And that means he's the one person who can tell me why my reclusive mother had Arcania's logo tattooed on her sole.

As a kid, I often badgered Mom about our lack of family. Didn't we have one aunt or uncle or cousin? Where was she born? Did her parents do something that made her cut ties? But she'd clam up every time or get upset and I backed down. How I wish now that I hadn't.

Had this place been a cult? Had Mom escaped? If so,

that would explain her obsessional fear about not being on social media, her hermit lifestyle, her never leaving the house. What if Mom's agoraphobia was deeply rooted in a past she fled?

I know next to nothing about the history of Arcania. My research at home hadn't given me much beyond the basics and I hadn't particularly cared, being swamped with grief and eager to get here to find out for myself the connection between Mom and a wellness retreat.

Now I wish I had access to the Internet to delve deeper. Though surely a place like this, steeped in rich history, would have that documented in a library?

I hadn't seen one on my original tour of the mansion, but I'd glimpsed floor-to-ceiling bookcases in the room marked Main Office when Cora had entered it this morning while I'd been on my way to breakfast.

If I expressed interest, would Cora allow me to research the history of this place?

Only one way to find out.

After downing the bottle of water on my bedside table, I check my watch and am surprised it's almost an hour since my run-in with Spencer at the tunnel and his strange proclamation I'm just like my mother. No good will come of me hiding in my room ruminating; time to see if I can discover more about Arcania.

Determined to discover Mom's link to this weird place, I stride toward Cora's office intending to peruse her library. When I reach her office, I raise my hand to knock, unsure whether I have the guts to enter if she's not here.

"Can I help you with something, dear?"

Cora's soft voice comes out of nowhere, and I jump. When I turn, she's right behind me, like she materialized out of thin air.

Her gaze is steady, but her pupils are tiny pinpricks. It's freaky. Is she on something?

Because I take too long to answer, she says, "Dear, is everything all right?"

Before I can nod, she reaches out and touches my arm. It's the faintest brush of her fingertips against my bare skin, but the cold clamminess of it gives me a jolt and I suppress a shudder.

"Yes, I'm fine, thanks. I was actually looking for you."

"Oh?"

Her eyebrows rise in unison, her skepticism easy to read, as if she knows I was contemplating sneaking into her office if she wasn't around.

"Yes. As you know, I work in a library back in Manhattan and I'm always drawn to the stories behind older stuff. Buildings, cities, that kind of thing, and the history of Arcania intrigues me. I was wondering if you had any books I can borrow to read up on it?"

She hesitates, before giving the slightest nod. "Of course, but if there's anything you want to know, all you have to do is ask."

Her expression is benign, serene, at complete odds with the spark of anxiety in her eyes.

"Actually, I wanted to ask Spencer too—"

"He's gone to visit family, so he'll probably be away until you leave." Her response is brusque and the worry lines between her brows deepen. "Maybe I can help?"

Stunned, I try to assimilate I'd barely seen Spencer sixty minutes ago and now he's left? Did Cora discover I'd been snooping and banished Spencer because of it? Or did he abscond of his own accord because he didn't want to answer my questions after his outlandish declaration about knowing my mother?

I could leave it alone, but I decide to call her on it. "Spencer's departure seems awfully sudden. I only spoke to him a little while ago."

Cora's glare is formidable. "The comings and goings of staff are of no concern to guests, dear. Now, are you still interested in those books?"

She's testy and definitely hiding something by her mutinous expression. But I'll get nowhere if I push her, so I appear suitably chastised and nod, relieved when Cora unlocks the office door before entering and beckoning me to follow.

"Was Arcania always a retreat?" I ask, not expecting Cora's laser-like focus to pin me like a moth to a corkboard.

"No. It started as an organic farm run by my in-laws many years ago." She slides a red leather-bound tome from a shelf, and a brown one from the shelf below it. "But I often wonder if the Norse ancestors of my husband viewed it as a refuge after their long months at sea."

"Were you a local? Is that how you met?"

Her expression blanks like shutters have been drawn. "No. I wasn't local." She thrusts the books at me so fast I almost stumble. "Here. These should give you a good feel for Arcania and the Outer Banks."

"Thanks."

The books are heavy and I shuffle their load to get comfortable. I should leave, but Cora's staring at me again like she can't quite figure me out and I wonder if I should ask her if she knew Mom like Spencer? Then again, with Mom having the same name as her dead daughter—and my sneaking suspicion they could be the same person and Mom faked her death to get away from here—asking Cora outright before I know more is foolhardy.

"Is there anything else you wanted, dear?"

I don't like being called dear. It may be a habit of Cora's, but it sounds faintly condescending the way she says it. I get the feeling she's toying with me, that she's humoring me by loaning me her precious books, but is hoping I don't probe too deep.

"No. I'll read these and let you know if I have questions."

"Please do," she murmurs, already turning away, but not before I glimpse genuine fear.

CHAPTER 18
CORA

T HEN

I'M CRADLING my baby daughter in one of the foyer's many nooks when Spencer approaches. My spine stiffens, as it inevitably does when we interact these days. It's been nine months since I married Harlan in an intimate ceremony in the orchard, a mere month after he proposed, with only his parents, Spencer, and Daphne in attendance. I fake smiled through the entire thing, reciting empty vows and pretending to stare at my husband in adoration.

His parents had been tight-lipped, and I still don't know what Harlan said to them to get them to approve of the marriage. I assumed he'd told them I was pregnant, and they didn't want an illegitimate child in the family.

I'd slept with Harlan the same day I accepted his outlandish proposal, ensuring that when my pregnancy was confirmed there was no question it was his.

Spencer asked me about the paternity once, the day after Harlan announced our engagement to everyone, but I reassured him Harlan was the baby's father and thankfully, my beautiful Ava had arrived two weeks late, so the timelines blurred.

I hate how I've hurt this man, because the moment I told Spencer I was marrying Harlan I saw the spark in his eyes die. But with Ava two months old now, I'm glad I made the decision I did. Being Harlan's wife gives me kudos and respect when I've never commanded either in my life. I'm besotted with Ava, as are her grandparents, and while I may not love my husband, I'm grateful for the stability our marriage provides.

When Spencer nears, I see he's ashen and dread settles like a rock in the pit of my stomach.

"What's happened? Is it Harlan?"

Spencer shakes his head. "There's been a boating accident. Magnus and Helga were the only ones onboard." His breath hitches and he blinks rapidly. "They're dead."

Shock makes me tighten my grip and Ava gives a soft mewl before settling again. "How did it happen?"

"There was an explosion..." He shakes his head. "Harlan's dealing with the police. He's taking care of everything."

Of course he is. For someone only a few years older than me, he's twenty-three going on forty. I've never met anyone so responsible.

"How is he?"

"Coping surprisingly well, though he broke down on the dock." Spencer grimaces. "Apparently he saw it happen."

A hint of foreboding tiptoes across the back of my neck. Harlan had told me he'd be spending the morning overseeing grafting in the orchard. What was he doing on the dock?

But I don't want to question Spencer and rouse his suspicions. Mine are bad enough. "How terrible for him."

"You know what this means, don't you?"

"What?"

"You and Harlan are now the new owners of Arcania." His gaze sweeps the foyer before settling on me again. "Congratulations."

I don't respond because I hate the tenuous connections my mind is making. Ever since we married, Harlan has been outlining plans for when he takes over Arcania. I've caught him poring over spreadsheets many times and found sketches of how he'd renovate and expand.

I'd made the mistake of teasing him once about his parents living another four decades, and he'd lost it. It's the only time he's ever raised his voice to me and he'd been instantly contrite, but that one glimpse at my husband's darker side showed the depth of his obsession with this place.

It makes me wonder; how far would he go to gain control of it?

"I'm still in my teens," I mutter, shaking my head. "Why would I care about running Arcania?"

Spencer hesitates, as if weighing up the wisdom of his next words. "Do you care about Harlan?"

I lower my gaze, a dead giveaway I can't look him in the eye and lie. "He's my husband. I have to care."

"That doesn't sound like a resounding declaration of love."

"Love's overrated. It's for fairytales."

"Yet you love Ava?"

"That's different," I snap, annoyed that he's trying to

trap me into saying something I shouldn't. "I'm going to put her down for a nap and go find Harlan."

When I stand, Spencer places a hand on my shoulder, and I hate the betraying sizzle that zaps through my body from his simple touch.

I miss our connection. Our banter. Our teasing. I'd deliberately shut all that down when I slept with Harlan in my quest to protect my unborn baby at all costs. I'd made my choice that day—choosing stability for my child over happiness for me—and I'd convinced myself I'd done the right thing. I had to, because every time I'd crossed paths with Spencer since, which is every freaking day, I silently lament how much I miss our camaraderie.

I see the way he looks at me sometimes, wistful and confused, and I hate it. I hurt him and he didn't deserve it. And the fact this his hand on my shoulder now feels comforting and right rather than the faintest revulsion I feel when Harlan touches me sometimes is a giveaway that no matter how many times I tell myself I've done the right thing for Ava, I'll always wonder 'what if' when it comes to Spencer.

"Just so you know, Harlan considers me his righthand man and I'm glad, because that means I'll always be here for you. Whatever you need, Cora, all you have to do is ask. As long as you're here, I'm sticking around." His squeeze his gentle. "I care about you, so know you can trust me. Always."

My heart pounds as our gazes lock and the sincerity in his makes tears spring to my eyes.

It's not lost on me I can barely summon sadness for the tragic death of my husband's parents, yet a kind word from Spencer makes me want to bawl.

"Thanks," I murmur, holding Ava to my chest. "That means a lot."

"Any time." He brushes a fingertip down Ava's cheek and the corners of her mouth curve upward.

I walk away before the tears fall.

CHAPTER 19

LUCY

I'm barely back in my room and nestled into the chintz armchair by the window with the first book, appropriately titled ARCANIA'S HIDDEN PAST, flipped to the foreword when there's a knock at my door.

Annoyed at the intrusion, I cross my bedroom and open the door.

"Hey, Lucy. You busy?" Demi asks, her smile genuine, and I subdue my first impulse to lie so I can be left alone.

"Just reading."

"Thought I'd pop by and let you know Cora's facilitating one of her impromptu meditation sessions. Our friends rave about them. Say they are life changing." She rolls her eyes. "I've never done one and personally, I doubt a few chants and deep breathing can achieve that much, but hey, we're here and it's part of the detox, so why not?"

I'm a skeptic like Demi, but with Spencer gone, Cora is my next go to for discovering Mom's connection here. Not that I'll ask her outright. There's something about Cora that makes me wary and I won't reveal my real reason for checking in to Arcania until I know more. What better way to get to know my hostess than attend her supposed life-altering meditation session?

"Count me in."

"Great." Demi claps her hands like an excited child. "Do you want me to wait for you or meet you in the yoga studio?"

"I need to change, so I'll see you there."

"Okay." Demi waves and practically jogs up the corridor, her jaunty ponytail swinging side to side, her matching peach leggings and crop top definitely designer. She makes me feel ancient when we're probably the same age.

Mid-twenties is young to be married these days, and it seems like Demi and Craig have been hitched for a while. They have that ease about them; not quite finishing each other's sentences, but a relaxed intimacy I envy.

I'm a librarian cliche, preferring the company of fictional men to the real thing. My infrequent lackluster dating lately hasn't inspired me to enter a committed relationship, let alone contemplate loving someone enough to marry.

In my teens, I blamed Mom for my non-existent social life; like her agoraphobia somehow rubbed off on me. I rarely got invited to parties and if I did, I'd end up with fellow nerds, pretending to enjoy the bitter beer but hiding behind a big red plastic cup staring wistfully at the popular kids dancing or making out.

Back then, it seemed easier to blame Mom than acknowledge the truth: that I'm not a people person and never will be. I'm inherently shy and cherish solitude.

Who knows, maybe it is more nurture than nature and growing up with Mom made me introverted? The thing is, I've been happy with my staid life. Until now. Losing Mom, then discovering her tattoo that points to a very different life she once had, has shaken me. It makes me question everything I've ever known. Am I wasting my life, feigning contentment when I should seek adventure? Is there more out there for me if I look for it?

Though I know myself. If my curiosity is piqued, I won't rest until I get answers, so I won't be able to move forward until I solve the mystery of Mom's link to Arcania. Maybe once that's done, I may shake things up? Take a long trip. Head overseas for the first time. See what the world has to offer beyond the Lower Manhattan Library and my brownstone that's so empty without Mom in it.

But for now, I'm here and I need to stop mulling over a bunch of 'what ifs' and focus on what's important: getting answers about Mom and getting closure. Not that I expect my grief to magically wane once I know how she's linked to this creepy place but my logical side that insists Mom's agoraphobia might be self-imposed in an effort to escape something or someone rather than psychological, will be appeased.

I've been absentmindedly staring at myself in the mirror while changing into yoga pants and a loose T-shirt, and I'm about to turn away when I glimpse something that makes me freeze.

In the middle of the awful green wallpaper behind my bed, bulging like its straining to escape the wall, is a face.

Not just any face.

It's Mom as a teen.

And her mouth is frozen wide in a silent scream.

CHAPTER 20
CORA

THEN

DAPHNE IS A GODSEND. I'm not sure what I would've done without her during the last three years. She's not just a superb cook, she's fantastic with Ava too and having a live-in nanny is a luxury I never take for granted. Thankfully, my beautiful daughter bypassed the terrible twos, and she's a happy, well-adjusted child who loves frolicking in the orchards, building sandcastles on the beach and helping Daphne bake.

She's clever too and I spend as much time as I can teaching her basic numeracy and literacy, and with her fourth birthday months off she's almost reading. I'd hoped she'd attend a preschool in Nag's Head, but the one time I mentioned it Harlan flew into a rage, making it more than clear Ava would be homeschooled, and I hadn't had the guts to broach the subject again.

I do that a lot these days, back away from a fight, and at twenty-two, when most people my age are at college or partying, I'm a shadow of the feisty, determined runaway I'd been when I first arrived at Arcania.

Then again, boldness is reserved for those without responsibility, those who can afford to take risks without consequences, and that's not me anymore. Ava is my priority and I'll continue to do whatever it takes to protect her. If that means pandering to my megalomaniacal husband, so be it.

Harlan's latest foible: he's hellbent on expanding Arcania. He wants to hire more workers and bring professional divers onboard.

Finding the priceless golden compass has become an obsession.

It doesn't help that we lose workers constantly. Harlan says they're greedy and dive unsupervised, hoping to steal his treasure, and probably drown. But if that's the case, why are their bodies never recovered? I assume they slip away in the night in search of alternative employment to escape my tyrannical husband; it never enters my head they drowned.

It's not the first time my husband's stories have raised my suspicions.

Initially, after his parents' death, he'd been inconsolable, but there'd been an unnatural quality to his grieving, almost like he could turn on the crocodile tears at will. In front of others, he played the part of a son who'd lost his parents in a tragic accident, but in private, he'd spend countless hours planning to make Arcania great.

When I asked him why he'd been on the dock that day, he said Magnus had noticed a fault in the fuel line and wanted Harlan to double check. According to my husband, there'd been nothing wrong with it, yet an investigation proved that had caused the explosion, and I couldn't help but wonder if Harlan deliberately sabotaged his parents' boat so he could assume power over Arcania.

It's a thought I couldn't shake at the time and it still haunts me, especially with the ongoing disappearances of our workers.

How far will Harlan go to fuel his obsession?

He's summoned me to his office, and when I enter, my heart sinks. Andreas, a worker who's been here for longer than me, is seated at a table.

With his tattooing equipment.

I know what this means. Harlan has made every employee go through the ritual of having the *vegvisir* tattooed on the sole of one of their feet to show loyalty to the cause: namely, finding the compass.

Initially, I couldn't believe how many of the workers gave in and got it done, until I figured that for many, they have no families or are running from something and this job, and the security it provides, is everything. Some consider it a lark, a way to show loyalty to the boss. I see it for what it is.

Harlan exerting his control over those who must serve him in his crazy quest.

I've avoided this ridiculous ritual by citing an excessive fear of needles, but by the determined look on my husband's face, he's not taking no for an answer any longer.

"Harlan, please—"

"It doesn't inspire the workers with confidence if you don't have the tattoo," he says, his steely tone brooking no argument. "You're my wife. Arcania is our legacy and Ava's birthright. You must get it done. This will be a symbol of belonging at Arcania for generations to come."

I'm not sure what scares me more: the sight of the needle in that damn machine about to pierce my skin repeatedly, the slight glaze in Andreas's eyes that suggests he's smoked weed before coming here, or Harlan's maniacal obsession.

I want to rant that I don't care about generations to come. That I don't care about this place. But he scored an indirect hit when he mentioned Ava's birthright.

My daughter is the reason I married Harlan. She's the reason I tolerate his idiosyncrasies and don't call him out on my suspicions regarding his parents' death and the regular disappearances of our workers. Ava is my world and I'll do anything to protect her, so if that means getting some stupid tattoo to appease my lunatic husband, I have no choice.

Harlan beams his approval when I slump in the chair beside Andreas, and he lifts my foot and rests it on the arm. I brace for the first prick of the needle, clenching my teeth so hard I'm surprised they don't crack. When the sting comes, it's excruciating and I cry out, squeezing my eyes shut and blindly reaching for Harlan's hand.

But I come up empty and when I open my eyes, Harlan's gone.

A FEW HOURS LATER, Spencer finds me curled up under my favorite tree in the orchard.

Our tree.

The one where he lay me down on a blanket that first time and made love to me.

It's my go-to comfort spot and I used to bring Ava here in the months after she was born, lying beside her on a picnic blanket, content just to watch her. The way her eyelids fluttered as she slept, her endless fascination with her toes, her gummy smiles. I never expected to love someone so completely. The kind of love I'd do anything to protect.

Which is why I need to keep a closer eye on my husband.

I don't like the change in his demeanor since he inherited Arcania. He's a demanding and controlling boss and I hear the whispers from the workers: they view him as a cult leader.

He has all the traits: charismatic, convincing, dominant, persuasive. He has an innate power to get people to do what he wants, like the workers who've never entered an ocean in their lives but are happy to learn to dive because Harlan presents his case in such a way they want to please him.

And he's bringing more people into the fold on the pretext of expanding the orchard. There's a lot more single employees now, men and women, who I can see are misfits. People like me when I first arrived here, craving a sense of belonging, of acceptance. Then there are the others, middle-aged and lonely, going through a transition in their lives, probably divorce, and they're particularly vulnerable as they latch onto stability, which belonging to the Arcania community provides.

I want to warn them it's a con. That Harlan doesn't care about them, that he's only using them to further his own agenda, that once they arrive they won't leave. I'm resigned to being stuck here. Having Ava has bound me to a man and a place I don't want. But my maternal instinct is strong and I'll do whatever it takes to ensure my daughter's safety.

Because I know if I ever try to run, Harlan will come after me.

He has the resources I don't and he'll find me and Ava, and I can't bear to think what he'll do to punish us.

"Are you okay?" Spencer sinks onto the blanket next to me. "You don't look so good."

"What every woman wants to hear," I mutter, and he laughs at my droll response.

"Seriously. Are you alright?" He brushes a strand of hair off my cheek and my breath hitches.

I make it a point not to be alone with Spencer like this because I'm susceptible to him. He genuinely cares about me and I'm so starved for affection I might do something rash.

"Harlan forced me to get the tattoo."

Spencer's eyes widen. "What do you mean by forced?" His jaw clenches and his hands curl into fists. "Did he hurt you?"

His protectiveness is heartwarming, but what can he do? If he ever challenges Harlan he'll be fired and then where will I be? I like having an ally in this place, someone I know will help me if I ever need it.

I shake my head. "No. But he knows I abhor needles, and he guilted me into it."

"I'm sorry." He reaches out to squeeze my hand, and I snatch it away.

"Please don't. If you touch me now, I may start bawling and never stop."

Sadness downturns his mouth. "We could run away. You, me, and Ava. Get as far from this place as humanly possible. I'll look after you. And I'll raise Ava as if she's mine—"

"Stop. Please." I barely squeeze the plea past the lump

of regret lodged in my throat. "You know him. He'd never stop until he found us and I don't trust him not to do something... drastic."

The resignation in Spencer's gaze matches mine because he knows I'm right. But this time when he reaches for me I don't stop him, as I sob into his shoulder and savor the comfort of his arms holding me tight.

CHAPTER 21

LUCY

I stare, transfixed, at the shimmery image of my mother reflected in the mirror, my throat constricted with terror.

I don't believe in ghosts and even if I did, why would Mom appear to me as a teenager?

I turn slowly, unsure whether I want to confront whatever this thing is—I don't believe it's Mom for a second because if she appeared to me it would be as a loving mother not this horrified vision with its mouth frozen open like some kind of Halloween mask—but when I glance at the wall, there's nothing there.

I blink several times, refocus, but the ugly green compass-embossed wallpaper is free of faces. Swiveling back to face the mirror, I brace in case it's some kind of weird reflective thing, but the vision I thought was Mom is gone.

Tears burn my eyes and I'm not sure if I'm more upset that what I saw was a figment of my overactive imagination or my curiosity about Mom's background has intertwined with grief, or that I'm projecting my sadness at losing Mom into bizarre illusions.

I press my fingertips to my eyes, willing the tears away. Spending time with fellow guests in Cora's meditation session is the last thing I feel like doing, but I know myself: hiding away here will only make me wallow and mull questions I may never get answers to.

Because that's the kicker in all this. What happens if I get to the end of this week and I haven't discovered how Mom and Arcania are linked?

I can't stay here indefinitely. I can't afford to and I'll lose my job. Then I'll be unemployed, unable to pay bills, and slowly losing my mind.

The emblem burned into my palm from the key fob and now, seeing Mom's face, is a worry. I'm practical rather than fanciful despite the paranormal books I devour by the truckload. I'm known at the library for my pragmatism. My co-workers appreciate it.

So what is it about this place that's making me see things that aren't real?

There's a soft knock at the door and I open it, to find Daphne holding a tray with a ghastly purple smoothie on it.

"The others have already had theirs and the meditation's about to get started, so I thought it'd be quicker if you drank yours here," she says, the lines fanning from the corners of her eyes deepening as she smiles.

"That's thoughtful of you," I say, eyeing the smoothie dubiously. "But what's in it? It looks radioactive."

She chuckles. "Beetroot. Guava. Ginger. Lemon. Agave syrup. Cora's a firm believer in nourishing the body and soul so all our guests get these before any of her sessions."

"Sounds healthy enough." I pick up the glass and take a

tentative sip, relieved when the concoction is palatable. "Thanks."

She's about to turn away when it hits me that I've been presented with the perfect opportunity. If Spencer's away, I can probe Daphne for information, considering she's worked here as long as him. It would've seemed odd for me to seek her out in the kitchen, but she's here now and I can't resist.

"Daphne, how long have you worked here?"

She pauses and turns back to face me, her expression wary. "Forty-two years."

"That's what Spencer said."

Her smile is barely perceptible. "We've been friends for a long time."

"You must love your job to stay so long."

"Arcania is home to me. I came here as a backpacking twenty-year-old and never left."

I struggle to hide my surprise. She's sixty-two? The deep grooves bracketing her mouth, the worry lines between her brows, and the map of wrinkles traversing her forehead date her to be at least a decade older.

"Cora must be a great boss because few people stay in one job that long."

Her nod is tentative, and she looks away. "I admire her. I witnessed firsthand how she stood up after losing her husband, then her daughter, and continued to run this place. It wasn't easy." She gives a little shake of her head. "We were all so close. I can't imagine the pain of losing Ava, but she was so stoic. It was a terrible business."

Daphne has been mute the few times I've encountered her so I'm definitely taking advantage of her garrulousness now.

"I heard an alligator took her daughter?"

"Yes. Ava always went on dawn walks. They found her favorite cap floating in the swamp. And a finger." Daphne shudders. "I avoided that spot for a year."

"How awful."

I swallow my disappointment. A body part, even a finger, being recovered at the scene means my suspicion is incorrect, because since I heard Mom and Cora's daughter had the same first name, a small part of me wondered if Mom had faked her death and escaped this place for whatever reason. That would make Cora my grandmother, and while the woman gives off some freaky vibes, it would be nice to have family beyond Mom.

With Daphne in a chatty mood, I continue to question her. "Were there other backpackers around when you first arrived here?"

She nods. "Lots. Magnus and Helga were renowned for hiring anyone passing through because their orchards were thriving. Plus there were many sunken treasure tales abounding that attracted adventure seekers."

"Sunken treasure?"

"Yeah. A famous Viking ship sunk off the coast close to here. That's how Arcania was built apparently, by the captain who made it ashore with gold filling his pockets. But there's rumored to be a priceless gold compass worth millions, along with coins, still aboard so many of the workers who stopped here got their diving certification so they could search the ruins."

My curiosity is piqued. Was Mom one of those adventure seekers? I know she had a fear of water so it's unlikely. Then again, what do I really know about Mom other than what I've observed firsthand growing up in our quiet household or what she told me, which isn't much, about her past?

"I saw Spencer in diving gear coming back from the beach the other morning. Does Cora still like her workers to search for the treasure?"

Daphne glances over her shoulder in inexplicable fear and takes a step back. "I must be going. I need to prepare lunch."

"But..." I trail off as I watch Daphne practically sprint up the corridor in the direction of the kitchen.

Bizarre, that she clammed up when I mentioned Cora.

What kind of hold does the owner of Arcania have over her employees and why are they fearful of her?

CHAPTER 22
CORA

T HEN

"Happy birthday, sweetheart." Harlan envelops Ava in a hug and I see my daughter stiffen. She's as wary of her father as I am. "I have a surprise for you."

"What is it, Dad?" Ava steps away when Harlan releases her and my heart sinks when his expression turns cunning.

I know what he has planned. I've protected Ava all these years from being branded, but she's eighteen today and I'd known deep down Harlan would force the issue.

"It's in here." He flings open the door to his office and the moment Ava sees Andreas with his tattoo paraphernalia, her startled gaze flies to mine.

I flash a brave smile when I'm dying on the inside. "It'll be okay, sweetie."

I slide my arm around her waist and squeeze, hating that she's trembling slightly. "I'm here."

"I don't want to do this, Mom." Her voice is barely above a whisper, but Harlan hears and his brows draw together in displeasure.

"Ava, you are an integral part of Arcania." He flings his arms wide. "This will all be yours one day and employees must see you're committed to seeing it thrive."

She rolls her eyes. "But who's going to see the sole of my foot, Dad?"

Every muscle in my body goes rigid. I've learned over the last umpteen years to never question my husband, to never talk back. It never ends well. Not that he's been physically violent, but the emotional and mental abuse is far worse. Bruises heal. Ongoing damage to my psyche, with him chipping away at it like a master trying to reveal what's in a block of marble, lasts forever.

I've kept Ava out of his way as much as possible. The only time Harlan interacts with his daughter is at dinner, which he insists is a formal occasion at the monstrous mahogany table in the dining room. Ava's clever and while I've never told her in as many words to avoid her father, she's learned to do just that. At dinner every night she's polite and fake smiles as much as I do, but I keenly observe how stilted she is, how tightly she grips her cutlery, how she flinches if he voices his displeasure over something trivial.

In comparison, she's affectionate with Spencer, and when I hear them laughing together in the orchard, it warms my heart and gives me pleasure in my dull life.

Spencer does that for me too, making my life brighter for fleeting moments. I'd resisted the inevitable—us resuming a relationship—for as long as I could, but on Ava's eighth birthday, after Harlan had deliberately belittled me in front of everyone at her party in the orchard then proceeded to ignore his daughter as if she'd done something wrong too, something inside me had snapped. So when Spencer sought me out on the beach later to comfort me, I'd succumbed and we've been secretly together ever since.

That's a decade ago, and I care about Spencer. Without him, I doubt I would've had the mental fortitude to survive my marriage and being a virtual prisoner in Arcania. But our assignations are always fraught, no matter how carefully we hide, and I live in perpetual fear of discovery.

Because we both know if Harlan ever finds out about our relationship, the consequences will be disastrous.

"Ava, you will not question me. This is happening whether you like it or not." Harlan's bristling with rage: his face is puce, his lips compress and the muscles in his neck are corded. "Now sit and let Andreas begin."

Andreas's eyes are lowered and I wonder if he remembers me being as recalcitrant eighteen years ago.

A shudder passes through Ava and I lean into her, wishing I could prevent this, hating my powerlessness. "I'm right here, sweetie. It won't take long."

"Mom. Please." Her eyes are wide with fright and nausea roils in my gut because her plea will go unheeded, because as much as I'd like to stop this, there's nothing I can do.

"I'm sorry," I mouth, and she knows it's over.

She has no choice.

The flash of fire in her eyes is more resignation than anger. She knows I'm a prisoner here as much as she is. She only asked me about leaving Arcania once and I broke down, sobbing so hard she joined in. The fact she does all her schooling online and has the occasional tutor if one of the workers has a talent in algebra or English means she learned from a young age that she lives in a gilded cage: shiny and pretty on the outside, dark and demonic on the inside.

Because that's what Harlan is, a narcissist possessed by a demon, his greed and quest for the compass knowing no bounds.

If he killed his own parents to get his hands on Arcania and employees continue to disappear, what will he do to us?

Ava is an empath and sensing my distress, she squares her shoulders, casts a malevolent glare at her father's back, and stalks toward Andreas. I want to go to her, to hold her hand, to offer whatever comfort I can, but Harlan bars my way when I take a step forward.

"She's eighteen, for goodness' sake. Stop mollycoddling her," he barks, only lowering his arm when he sees my brief nod of acceptance.

I wince at the first prick of the needle on Ava's sole and clamp my lips shut when I see her lower lip wobble. There are tears in her eyes, but she's defiant, glaring at her father the entire time, refusing to let them fall.

Our gazes lock and I hope she can read the message in mine.

That's my girl.

CHAPTER 23
LUCY

I'm sipping the last of my purple smoothie when I enter the yoga room. Craig and Demi are already sitting on mats and Cora, standing at the front of the room, casts me a disapproving glare.

"Sorry I'm late," I mumble, downing the rest of my drink before choosing a mat at the back.

Cora ignores my apology and claps her hands once, loudly. "Let's get started. Lie on your backs. Close your eyes. Blank your mind."

Sounds like a run-of-the-mill meditation so far and nothing like the transformational experience Demi mentioned her friends had. Then again, I'm not Cora's greatest fan because there's something about her I don't like, so I'm skeptical.

Cora's voice drones on: focus on tensing and releasing individual muscle groups from our toes to our head, concentrate on pushing air deep into our lungs, exhaling to a slow count. Your generic meditation session, and I'm pleasantly drowsy when I hear it.

Mom's voice.

Let me go. Please. I'm begging you.

I can't stay here.

You know what happens when you step out of line.

It doesn't matter who I am.

I'll be killed like the rest of them.

My eyes snap open as a cold sweat breaks out over my body. My pulse races as I stare at the ceiling, stunned to see a vision of my mother as a teen running along the path to the beach, her long blonde hair streaming behind her.

I blink and refocus, and this time she's in the foyer, patting the walls like she's seeking an escape route. When she glances over her shoulder, the sheer terror on her face makes my breath catch.

I sit bolt upright, my heart pounding so loud I can hear it. Craig and Demi have vanished, while Cora is lying on a mat at the front of the room, staring at the ceiling.

Did she see what I did? Or is my quest for answers about Mom sending me completely loopy?

As if sensing my distress, Cora's head rolls to the side until her gaze fixes on me. I expect her to stand and approach me and ask what's wrong. Or to tell me to lie down again.

Instead, our eyes lock for the scantest second before she resumes looking upward. But not before I've seen the oddest thing.

A smug smile playing about her lips.

CHAPTER 24
CORA

T HEN

AVA HASN'T BEEN the same since she got tattooed two months ago.

She's tougher now and I observe her petty acts of rebellion without outright condoning them. Harlan's keys go missing, shipping orders get messed up, and one of his prized apple trees won't produce anymore. I suspect she's sabotaged it somehow but cleverly, so suspicion isn't thrown on any of the workers.

That's another thing that's changed. Harlan expects her to work now. He flatly refused my pleas for her to go to college, despite the many ways I presented logical arguments: like how a business degree could only benefit Arcania in the long run, how a marketing degree could help promote Arcania, how an economics degree would ensure she preserved the legacy he was creating.

Nothing worked, and a small part of me I daren't acknowledge was actually relieved. If Ava left, I'd be all alone with a monster.

So Ava is doing a remote degree in business management from a local community college while working in the orchards. She appears oddly upbeat the last week and I'm assuming it has something to do with the young tradesmen who are renovating some of the rooms.

Harlan has a hare-brained idea to turn Arcania into a bed-and-breakfast some time in the future, when the last thing I want is a bunch of strangers traipsing through our house.

I know what's behind his idea. With the huge turnover of orchard workers—thanks to their 'leaving'—I suspect he wants to convince guests about the validity of sunken treasure and somehow get them invested.

It's crazy, but I've learned not to voice my opinion these days. It never ends well. We sleep in separate rooms these days. Heck, we barely converse. I was a means to an end. He wanted to show his parents how he could be a stable family man to ensure he inherited Arcania, and once they were gone, he didn't have to pretend any longer.

I don't mind. I prefer it this way. Because technically, while I'm cheating on Harlan with Spencer, I wouldn't have rekindled our relationship if my marriage was healthy. We'd been platonic for a year before Ava's eight birthday, when I'd turned to Spencer for comfort because of Harlan's callous indifference to his daughter and slept with him.

I know what I'm doing is wrong. I feel guilty at times, because Spencer gets nothing out of our arrangement. We can never parade our relationship in public. I can never acknowledge how much he means to me. But he's reassured me many times that he's content with the status quo and I choose to believe him because I'd be bereft without him. Selfish of me, but I need one ally in this place.

I've seen Ava conversing with one young tradesman in particular, an electrician who channels laid-back surfer vibes: dirty blonde hair spiked in all directions, bright blue eyes, amiable smile, tanned. I want to warn her that if her father sees her he won't approve, but my heart is lighter when I see her genuinely smile for the first time in ages, so I remain silent. It's healthy for her to talk to boys, to flirt, to have some sense of normality in her sheltered world.

I hate to think too far ahead—how will she meet a man to cherish her, who will she marry, will she bring children into this weird world we inhabit—so I don't.

Which is why when she comes to me on this gloomy day while I'm waking on the beach, I know something is wrong. I feel it in my bones. The terror on her face, the wringing of her hands, the frequent glancing over her shoulder, means she has to tell me something and it can't be good.

"Ava, what is it?" I grasp her upper arms, hoping to infuse her with strength. "You can tell me anything."

She gnaws on her bottom lip, unable to meet my eyes. I give her arms a gentle squeeze and she finally drags her gaze upward.

When I see regret, fear and hope, I don't know what to think.

"Ava?"

"I'm pregnant, Mom."

Three little words that drop a bomb into our midst, a detonation I know will have far-reaching consequences.

CHAPTER 25

LUCY

T he rest of the meditation session is uneventful—
Craig and Demi reappeared shortly after my
bizarre vision—but the last thing I feel like doing
is relaxing after what I saw and heard. As an isolated inci-
dent, I wouldn't be worried, but seeing and hearing Mom
everywhere I turn here is disconcerting.

Okay, it's more than that, but I'm playing down my
abject terror that this place has a weird hold over its inhabitants. Maybe it's not Cora I have to worry about as much as
what's within the walls of Arcania itself?

I wait until Demi and Craig leave before approaching
Cora.

"How did you find that, dear?" She beams at me like she
didn't see me quietly freaking out in the middle of her
session. "Many find it transcendental."

"So you rarely have your guests standing in the middle
of a session because they're freaked out by seeing stuff on
the ceiling?"

She arches her brow. "I saw you stand, but I assumed
you had a back spasm, which is not uncommon in some

who lie on hard ground for a period of time and need to stretch."

She peers at me like she can't figure me out. Ironic, as that's exactly how I feel about her. "What did you see?"

Alerting her to the real reason I'm a guest in this whacky place isn't on my agenda, so I fake a yawn. "I think I drifted off for a second and must've had a nightmare."

She leans closer, and I don't like the maniacal gleam in her eyes. "But what did you see?"

"Someone falling in front of a bus."

The lie slides easily from my lips because I have had that precise nightmare ever since I learned how Mom died.

"Oh dear, that sounds dreadful." She reaches out and touches my arm, and once again I struggle not to flinch from her icy fingers. "Perhaps you'd benefit from a one-on-one session with me? I'm not a trained psychologist, but I've done several courses and guests often find it soothing to talk to me. I'm an excellent listener."

The only thing I want to talk to this batty lady about is my mom, but that's not going to happen until I find out more. Once I'm armed with more solid evidence Mom stayed here and was so connected to the place she had its emblem tattooed on her foot, I'll confront Cora.

"Do you ever give guests access to the Internet?"

Cora frowns. "The whole point of coming here is to digitally detox. So no cells, no television, no computers. Weren't those books I gave you informative enough?"

Not nearly enough information—not the kind I need— so I say, "They're interesting, but I'm more fascinated by the history of Arcania specifically rather than Flotilla Firth and would love to delve deeper while I'm here rather than waiting until I get home."

"Obsession is as harmful as being addicted to screens,"

she says, her lips compressed in a thin line. "If those books I gave you aren't enough, there should be another in your room about the historical significance of this place."

"Actually, it's a general history of the Outer Banks, whereas, as I've already said, I'm more interested in Arcania."

"Why?" Her voice rises slightly and anger lights her eyes.

Strange, because I'd think an owner of a mansion so obviously steeped in history wouldn't mind talking about it or assuaging a guest's curiosity.

"Because old houses fascinate me." I reach for another lie.

She pins me with an accusatory glare, and I struggle not to squirm under her scrutiny. "Then you can wait until you get home to research us."

"But I've just told you—"

"Enough," she yells, and I jump. "We don't like people prying, so you'll be best served to stop badgering. It won't end well."

She's shouting and I'm open-mouthed as her face flushes crimson. "You need to retire to your room." She pauses, her glower formidable. "Now."

How she makes her last order sound so ominous I'll never know and as I take a step back, I glimpse movement out of the corner of my eye. Great, that's all I need, another weird vision. But when I half turn, I see Craig and Demi just inside the door, wearing the same shell-shocked expressions I'm sporting.

Cora follows my line of vision and the moment she sees the couple have witnessed her meltdown, the tension marring her face is erased in an instant.

"I advise everyone to go to their rooms and have a rest

after one of my sessions," she says, her tone soothing and at complete odds with the way she yelled at me a few moments ago. "And if you don't feel like having lunch in the dining hall, I'll arrange to have Daphne bring it to your rooms."

She doesn't wait for a response and strides from the studio with her head held high, like we haven't just had a terrifying glimpse into her psyche beneath the serene exterior.

Demi approaches me as Craig glances after Cora, his expression puzzled.

"Are you okay?" Demi asks. "She seriously lost it."

"And she virtually threatened you," Craig adds.

I want to confide in this couple. They've been nothing but lovely since we met. But I don't trust easily and telling them the truth may result in Cora clamming up completely if they leak why I'm really here.

"I'm fine," I say. "Though that was seriously freaky."

Demi and Craig nod in unison. "We only came back because Craig thought he'd left his water bottle behind," Demi says, shaking her head. "She glared at us earlier when we snuck out for a toilet break halfway through the session, but her annoyance then is nothing on what we just witnessed." A slight frown mars Demi's perfectly smooth brow. "It's strange how a person can present a perfect front until something sets them off."

"Yeah," I say, wondering why Cora is so over-protective of Arcania. It's not like I was asking to renovate the mansion, I just want to know more about the history.

"For someone who perpetuates relaxation and detox-ing, how she yelled at you was way out of line." Craig frowns. "I've worked with people like that before and their instability can be toxic."

"So your friends who've stayed here before have mentioned nothing about Cora?"

He shakes his head. "We wouldn't be here if they had. We came her to de-stress, not to be threatened by some psycho."

Demi lays a comforting hand on his forearm. "That's harsh, babe."

Considering I saw flecks of spittle flying from Cora's mouth when she yelled at me, I don't think so.

I'd come here to get answers—and if I'm completely honest, as a distraction from my grief—but nothing about Arcania has helped. I'm seeing things, hearing things, and have now unintentionally invited the wrath of Cora upon myself. It's too much and I'm momentarily lightheaded.

"Hey, you need to rest." Demi threads her arm through my left elbow, Craig my right, and they gently lead me from the studio. "If I were you, I'd lie down for a bit, then lodge a formal complaint."

"Who to? Cora owns this place," Craig mutters.

I sense rather than see her shooting her husband a look over my head. "It can't hurt to put it in writing. At the very least, she owes you an apology."

"And if she doesn't say sorry, we'll back you up in your complaint," Craig says. "The last thing she'd want is for us to leave bad reviews when we leave and finally have access online again."

"I'll think about it," I murmur, relieved when we reach my room. I'm glad for their support because my legs are decidedly wobbly and my head is still spinning a little. "Thanks for walking me back, guys, and for the support. I appreciate it."

"Anytime." Demi gives me a quick hug and Craig

squeezes my shoulder in silent support. "Rest up. And let us know if you need anything."

Considering there are no phones in the rooms, I'm not sure how I'll do that, but it's the thought that counts.

"We'll see you later," Craig says, with a half-wave, and as they stroll down the corridor toward the foyer, I see Cora watching us before she slips out of sight.

Weary to my bones, I insert the key into the lock and turn the knob. But it sticks and I jiggle it, yelping when the skin on my palm burns at the knob's sudden heat.

I snatch my hand away, biting my lower lip to stop from crying. Not from the unexpected pain but from being over-whelmed by this house and the bizarre happenings.

The skin on my palm is unblemished and when I tenta-tively touch the knob with a finger, it's cool to my touch. I quickly open the door and all but stumble into my room before slamming the door shut behind me.

The curtains have been drawn so the room is shrouded in darkness and as my eyes adjust to the gloom, I freeze.

Someone is sitting in the chair by the window.

CHAPTER 26
CORA

T HEN

"YOU HAVE TO TRUST ME, CORA." Spencer hauls me into his arms and hugs me tight. "I'll take care of this."

I struggle out of his embrace, icy fear trickling through me at what Spencer may do to protect Ava and me. Even the calmest man can be pushed to his limits, and I dare not contemplate how far Spencer will go for me. He's devoted and if pushed to the edge... but he's nothing like my sadistic husband and I must keep the faith.

"What do you mean, you'll take care of this?"

"It's not what you're thinking." Disappointment down-turns his mouth that even for a second I'd think badly of him. "I would never pressure Ava into terminating."

"But when Harlan finds out she's pregnant..." I shiver, unable to shake the chilling fear that's dogged me ever since Ava told me the news yesterday. "I'm scared of what he'll do to her."

"To both of you." He cups my cheek and I lean into his hand. "We know he'll somehow find a way to blame you for this." His lips compress and the tender glint in his eyes hardens. "I won't let him do anything to harm either of you."

I want to believe in Spencer so badly. I like to think he has the power to go up against someone like Harlan. But a small part of me knows these are empty promises. What can Spencer do against the might of Harlan?

"Will you be okay?" He envelops me in his arms and I nod against his chest.

"Thanks for always being here for me," I murmur, and he strokes my head in response, smoothing my hair in comforting rhythmic caresses that allow me to believe for a few brief moments that he's right and everything will work out.

But all too soon he releases me, and I head back to the house. As I enter, I hear raised voices from the second floor, and my blood freezes. Harlan is ranting, yelling 'whore' and 'slut', and I take the stairs two at a time.

As I reach the top landing, Ava rushes past me, tears streaming down her face as she descends the stairs and disappears out the front door.

I want to go after her, but I need to deal with my husband first. He can't treat Ava like that.

"Don't you ever call our daughter filthy names again." I jab my finger in his direction, fear making my hand shake as he advances toward me.

"Did you know?"

I tilt my chin up, not giving him the satisfaction of seeing how much he intimidates me. "Know what?"

"Don't play dumb with me." He backhands me so fast I stagger, grateful for the railing against my back so I don't fall at his feet. The pain is blinding and I blink rapidly so I can avoid another hit, or worse. My cheek throbs in time with the blood pounding in my ears as a fury I've never experienced before fills me.

It's the first time he's struck me and, in a warped way, it gives me power. Now I have an excuse to set my rage free.

"Do both of you think I'm an idiot? She didn't touch her wine last night at dinner and now I find her throwing up for the second morning in a row because of a 'virus'." He makes inverted comma signs with his fingers. "Why didn't you tell me she was pregnant?"

"It's not my place to tell you—"

He hits me again, this time an open slap to the side of my head. I'm dizzy for a moment, reeling from the impact, as my mouth fills with the coppery taste of blood, but something inside me snaps.

"Does hitting me make you feel better, Harlan? Because if so, go ahead, get it out of your system, because I'll make sure you never lay a finger on our daughter."

Surprise widens his eyes. "What are you talking about?"

"I know you killed your parents. I know you make workers who steal gold from the shipwreck disappear. And I'll be damned if something happens to Ava."

I'm yelling, sweat trickling down my back, my body so hot I feel like I could combust at any second.

In contrast, Harlan's deadly cool alerts me I've gone too far. "So you know huh?" He slow claps, his creepy grin making me take a step sideways so I can bolt down the stairs if needed. "Well done, detective. Surely you've learned by now I can do anything I want and nobody can stop me?"

He throws his arm wide, encompassing this oppressive house. "I'm the only one who can take Arcania to the next level, to the greatness it deserves. And no whoring daughter of mine will taint its name."

"I said don't call her that."

I take a step forward, and he has the audacity to laugh in my face.

"It's no great surprise, really. Her mother's a whore, stands to reason Ava inherited that from you."

His upper lip curls in a sneer as he turns his back on me and descends the first step.

Red spots dance before my eyes, blurring my vision. I let the rage expand into every cell of my body, and my muscles twitch and flex, ready to fight.

I swear I lift out of my body and I'm looking down on myself as I place my hands in the middle of his back and push. Hard.

Detached, I watch him tumble down the stairs.

I savor every bump, every crack, every snap, until he's lying in a crumpled heap at the bottom, his eyes open and glassy.

And I don't feel a flicker of remorse.

CHAPTER 27

LUCY

My fingers tremble as I pat the wall in search of the light switch, and when I flick it, I'm relieved to find the person sitting in the chair by the window isn't human. It's a diving suit propped up, complete with an archaic helmet that nobody has used to dive in a century.

I've never been out of New York, but I attended a library conference on Long Island once, so I know it's perfectly normal for hotel staff to enter guest rooms to clean and replenish bathroom supplies.

But why would a staff member leave me a diving suit when I've never expressed an interest in the water sport?

Not that I'd ever try it. I've inherited Mom's fear of the ocean and have never been near it. With Mom never leaving the apartment, I didn't feel like traveling on my own. That conference was the one and only time I'd been away from her for more than a night and I'd stayed away from the Atlantic despite it almost lapping at the hotel's back door.

Here, I can hear the ocean if I leave my window open. I did it the first night I arrived and despite my inherent fear

131

of the tides, I found the rhythmic crashing of waves soothing.

That first morning when I'd encountered Spencer, he'd been diving. Is this some prank he's pulled to reinforce his warning for me to leave this place?

But Spencer has gone to visit family according to Cora and even if he was around, would he do something so freaky?

Daphne seems perfectly normal and had been happy to converse earlier until I mentioned her boss. And the other guests wouldn't have access to my room.

So that leaves Cora. But what would she gain by spooking me? I'm a paying customer and she doesn't have a clue why I'm really here.

Whoever it is, they're messing with the wrong person. I don't scare easily—unless it involves large bodies of water —and I'll do anything to solve the mystery of Mom's attachment to this place.

I approach the diving suit cautiously—with what's been happening in this place, I half expect it to come alive and leap at me—and draw back the curtains. If I had a phone, I'd call Cora to ask her who did this, but I'm exhausted to my bones and all I want to do right now is lie down.

I down a bottle of water, turn off the light, and slide between the covers, allowing the strange lethargy stealing over me since the end of Cora's meditation session to take over.

It usually takes me ages to fall asleep, so I don't know how long I've napped for when I finally wake. My eyelids are heavy and I rub my eyes before opening them.

To find the diving suit gone.

CHAPTER 28
CORA

T HEN

N<small>O ONE SUSPECTS ME</small>. They believe Harlan fell down the stairs. Only Ava casts me sideways glances when she thinks I'm not looking, but I can tell she's more relieved than accusatory. The funeral is low key. It's no surprise Harlan was so disliked he had zero friends. Now I'm the mistress of Arcania and I'm determined to purge his presence from our home.

But the house has other ideas.

Whenever I sit at his desk, I feel the walls closing in on me. Every room is suffocating, like a blanket of humidity smothers everything. Random items fall from the shelves—books, a candle, a miniature bronze bust—and cold air sweeps over me at the oddest of times.

I don't believe in ghosts but if I did, I'd swear Harlan is

trying to make my life a misery, even more than he did when he was alive.

Then I find his diary.

It's a small, dog-eared, black leather journal tucked beneath old ledgers in the bottom drawer of his desk. There's not much in it. A few random entries, mostly about the history of Arcania, but his jottings on the last page prove enlightening.

He believed a legend. Lived it, to the extent everything he did around here was controlled by his belief.

He saw visions in the house's walls. Visions of his parents, of employees, of a gleaming gold shipwreck.

He heard voices, demanding he assume control of Arcania and all who lived here.

He dived repeatedly because he believed that finding the gold compass was the only way to appease the angry Norse gods.

It became his obsession.

I would never be like that.

But over the next few weeks, I question my sanity and I, too, would do anything to make the strange occurrences in this house go away.

I'm in the middle of a meditation that's doing little to soothe my disturbed soul when Spencer enters the room.

I've avoided him since Harlan's death because I know if I let him get too close, I'll blurt out the truth surrounding my husband's demise and I'm not telling anyone. I'm taking that secret to the grave.

"Cora," he whispers, and every hair on my body snaps to attention.

There's sorrow in his voice, underlined with devastation, and I know in my gut only one thing could make him sound like that.

Something's happened to Ava.

I stretch slowly and accept the hand he holds out to pull me to my feet.

"Did Ava miscarry?" I ask, a petty part of me annoyed Ava would go to Spencer before me.

He shakes his head, and when he lifts it, I see the tears coursing down his cheeks.

Dread blooms in my chest. "What's happened?"

He opens his mouth to speak, but no sound comes out. Until an awful wail makes me yank my hand out of his and step back.

"Spencer, you're scaring me."

He whispers her name. "Ava..."

My chest tightens, and I have trouble breathing. "What about Ava?"

I know before he responds this is going to be bad. It's going to be far worse than anything I've had to cope with in my entire life.

"She's gone."

All the air whooshes out of my lungs in relief. My daughter has finally left Arcania. I've been expecting it, but I wish she'd told me. Though I'm sure she'll reach out once she's settled somewhere; probably to ask for money.

But why is Spencer so bereft?

"An alligator in the swamp took her..." he starts sobbing, so I have difficulty computing his words. "Her hat and a finger were all that remained."

I don't hear anything else but I feel it.

The darkness.

Pressing in on me.

Until I give myself over to it and feel nothing at all.

CHAPTER 29
LUCY

I don't leave my room for the rest of the day. Daphne brings me dinner—a ridiculously healthy poke bowl filled with brown rice, quinoa, hummus, cabbage, and peas sauteed in garlic, sprinkled liberally with black sesame seeds—but doesn't stay despite my efforts to draw her into conversation. Instead, she leaves the tray and bolts. It seems that woman is afraid of her own shadow but she'd been so normal when we chatted earlier.

While I eat, I flip through the Outer Banks history book. As expected, it's a broad summary of the area, with scant mentions of sunken ships and nothing about Arcania. Flotilla Firth, where Arcania is located, literally means small navy fleet in a sheltered inlet, but the historical significance mentions nothing about the navy and is heavily populated by pirate tales. It's fifty miles from Nag's Head, which got its name from land pirates placing a lantern around the neck of an old horse, a 'nag', and leading it along the dunes so that ships out at sea saw it. Thinking it was a gently bobbing boat in a sheltered cove, the captain would seek a safe harbor, but the boat would run aground on the sharp shoals near the shore and the land pirates would pillage the ship.

It's a fascinating tale and I'm so engrossed I forget to eat. This often happens at home when I'm entranced by a book and Mom would chastise me... I blink and stare at the poke bowl. Mom isn't around anymore and in that moment I'm swamped by a wave of loneliness so strong I wrap my arms around my middle.

I'll never hear her soft laugh as she watches sitcom reruns.

I'll never taste her incredible Irish stew I can't master, no matter how many times I try.

I'll never see that indulgent look on her face, the one where I'd catch her watching me unawares, like she couldn't believe how lucky she was to have me.

Sorrow clogs my throat and I pick up a fork and spoon the rice into my mouth to dislodge it. I need to eat. I can't afford to feel woozy like I did earlier, because with Cora's over the top reaction today, I feel like I'm getting somewhere. If I can push her buttons a little more, who knows what I may discover?

I continue to read as I demolish the delicious rice, followed by a simple fruit salad of orange, watermelon, apple, and pear. There are extensive chapters on the piracy in this region and I flip through them, before seeing something that catches my eye.

The *vegvisir*.

Interestingly, the Viking compass doesn't date back to the Viking era, in the eighth to eleventh centuries. It came into being much later in Europe and the Nordic people claimed it as their own because if they carried the sign, that person would never lose their way in storms or bad weather, even when the route was unknown.

Is that why Mom had the compass tattooed on her sole? To protect her and guide her home? But if so, Arcania is her sanctuary, yet she never once mentioned it to me. And she obviously left without looking back.

Nothing about this place suggests a haven to me. It's too creepy. Too many shadows, too many nooks. As for those tunnels that run beneath the mansion, who knows what lives down there?

I know I'm being fanciful. Which budding writer isn't? Those tunnels are more than likely linked to the piracy centuries ago that I just read about. And if a house has a spooky aura, it doesn't mean anything nefarious lingers within its walls.

I need to focus on facts. My mother had Arcania's logo tattooed on her foot. That's why I came here, to discover how that happened; I should ignore the rest of the mysterious stuff.

I read on, desperate to discover all I can about the *vegvisir*. According to legend, the symbol was drawn onto the traveler's forehead before leaving home.

In blood.

A chill sweeps over me and I look up from the book to find my room shrouded in darkness, bar the lamp I'm using to read. I stand to draw the curtains and as I glance outside, I see what looks like a thousand lanterns bobbing in the trees. Considering the few people staying here, that can't be right, so I blink several times but the lights are still there, constantly moving.

I crack the window but can't hear anything, bar the distant boom of the ocean's waves crashing against rocks. As I close the window, I see the lights coalesce into the symbol I've just been reading about.

Impossibly, the *vegvisir* is suspended high about the

trees, floating in nothingness, its vivid turquoise lighting the sky momentarily, before it vanishes.

I rub my eyes and refocus, continuing to look out the window in the hope I'll see something that makes sense, something to justify these crazy visions I keep having. But there's nothing.

I must be more overtired than I thought, despite my nap earlier. Maybe a good night's sleep will diminish these weird notions that plague me. It's not the first time reading about something otherworldly has made my imagination run wild.

But those other times were different. I'd had dreams and this time, staring out the window, I'd been very much awake.

I close the book and slide it back onto the bookshelf before placing my tray outside my door. Bed is beckoning, for no other reason than I may get some reprieve from the endless thoughts and questions pinging through my head.

I expect to lie awake for a long time considering my nap, but I drift off quickly. Only to be woken by the sound of thundering hooves.

I open my eyes, expecting the noise to stop. That's what happens with dreams. But the pounding is relentless and I sit up in bed, immediately wishing I hadn't when I see people in white robes running mindlessly in circles, their terror palpable.

So not a dream then, a nightmare. But my room looks exactly how it was before I fell asleep, apart from the galloping hooves and the robed people.

I inhale deeply, taking in great lungfuls of air, before exhaling slowly. Over and over. Hoping to calm my nerves. There's a difference between being edgy because I'm sleep deprived and grieving and feeling like this house is coming alive and deliberately scaring me.

The robed people meld into the wall and disappear, only to be replaced by my mother running through the tunnel I'd explored, abject terror contorting her face. Her mouth is wide open in a silent scream and she's scrabbling at the stone walls until her fingers bleed.

My chest is so tight I can't breathe, and I claw at the blankets covering me, desperate for air. Goosebumps cover my arms as Mom fades into the wall too, her eyes locking on mine before she disappears.

That's when the moaning starts, followed by a low growl of "Help me, Lucy. Help me."

Trembling, I leap out of bed and stumble to the door. I need to get out of here. I flick the lock, fumbling with the knob as fear courses through me. The doorknob is rigid and I yank at it repeatedly until it suddenly gives and the door flings open, sending me slamming against the wall behind it.

My bones rattle and the back of my head throbs with the impact, but it doesn't stop me.

I stagger into the corridor and make a run for it.

CHAPTER 30
CORA

T HEN

My grief is overwhelming.

I lose track of time. Hours meld into days, days into weeks, weeks into months. I drift through the house like a ghost, unseeing, uncaring. Chills wrack my body and no amount of stoked fires or blankets can warm me. The orchards wither because the workers leave in droves. Nobody wants to come near us because they believe Arcania is cursed. Rumors abound.

I don't care about any of it because my life as I know it is over. Fate is sadistic. I thought I'd saved Ava by getting rid of Harlan, only to have her cruelly snatched from me. I'd warned her about the boardwalk, how I never took a stroll along it because the swamp harbored a malevolent presence the same as the house. But my daughter didn't listen and now I'm alone.

Daphne and Spencer stay, though I can't rely on them. As the mistress of Arcania I need to establish boundaries now and that means treating Daphne as a cook and Spencer as housekeeper/manager. Whatever relationship Spencer and I had that might've developed into something more is now over. I'm not the same person and it's not just the grief gnawing away at me every day.

I've come to a decision.

My entire life, I've never belonged anywhere. Mom and her transient boyfriends made me feel unwelcome, and even when I married Harlan I felt like his instability could undermine me at any moment and I'd be homeless again.

So I've quelled my initial urge to sell this place and get as far from Arcania and its terrible memories as I can, and have decided to stay and transform it.

Wipe away the past.

Focus on the future.

Make Arcania great again.

Harlan was a greedy narcissist whose obsession with a legend made him lose sight of what he had: a magnificent house and impressive surroundings that can be changed into anything. So that's what I'm going to do. Make Arcania welcoming. Entice people to visit, to fill the rooms with love and laughter and help me banish the ghosts.

Money isn't an issue thanks to Harlan's careful investments with the income from the orchard over the years, so I'll renovate. A complete refurbishment with the view of potentially listing Arcania as a B&B.

I can do this.

Darkness descends quickly in Flotilla Firth and as I stare out the window from my office, I see a light bobbing along the boardwalk. I stiffen, because it can only be

Spencer or Daphne and I assume neither is foolish enough to walk alongside the swamp in the dark.

My fingernails dig into the windowsill as the light draws nearer and I blink. My mind is playing tricks on me because for a moment I see Ava. Wishful thinking, as Spencer materializes and I realize in that moment how in the right light, with shadows shrouding him and his head tilted at an angle as he glances over his shoulder, how much Ava looks like him.

I've seen a slight resemblance over the years but dismissed it for fear if I could see it Harlan might too, but maybe I'd been looking for things that weren't there, a reminder that no matter how much my husband thought he controlled me, my daughter was the biggest rebellion.

Spencer reaches the front door and I know it's time.

Time to tell him my decision.

I open my office door as he enters the foyer. The gloom is omnipresent, but I can't see the point in lighting the place with only three of us here.

His gaze lands on me, silhouetted in the doorway, and the tenderness I see in his eyes makes my resolve wavers. For years we've had to hide our relationship. He's been my rock and asked nothing of me. He's stoically supported me and Ava, and now with Harlan gone, I know Spencer will assume our relationship can finally flourish.

I assume he'll leave when I make a clean break and while I'll miss him, I need to do this. Rely on no one. Cleanse my grief by reinvigorating Arcania. It's the only way forward. Because as much as I care about Spencer, I don't love him. At least, not enough to give up the one thing that provides me with stability: this place.

"Can we talk?" I ask, stepping aside so he can enter the office.

I've deliberately chosen my office as the place to break the news to him as it's more professional and he knows it by the slight elevation of his brow as he passes me.

"Everything okay?" His hand lingers in the small of my back for a few moments, and I grit my teeth against the urge to lean into him.

It would be so easy to give in and become the couple he wants to be, but I must remain resolute.

"As okay as it can be when my reason for living is dead."

He nods, sorrow down turning his mouth. "I miss Ava too, every damn day."

I refrain from pointing out it's not the same, that I'm her mother. Then again, I wonder if Spencer saw through my lie when he questioned Ava's paternity all those years ago and knows she was his.

"What I'm about to say may sound harsh, but you need to hear it." I consider sitting for a moment, but that will imply comfort and nothing about this impending confrontation is comfortable. "I'm sorry, Spencer, but our relationship moving forward must be strictly platonic."

His eyes widen in shock and his lips part as he takes a step toward me, but I hold up my hands to ward him off.

"I'll understand if you want to leave and I'll miss you, but this is my decision."

He shakes his head. "Why? What's changed?"

"Apart from the fact my daughter is dead, you mean?"

Sorrow darkens his eyes. "You can lean on me, you know. I'm grieving too."

"This isn't about my grief. It's about me finally doing something on my own, standing on my own two feet, without needing anybody."

His lips thin. "There's a difference between independence and foolhardiness." He points to himself. "Haven't I

144

always been here for you? Supported you?" His face flushes crimson. "Loved you?"

The burgeoning ache in my chest spreads until I can barely breathe. I hate having to hurt this amazing man. "You know I care for you. I always have."

I pause and see the exact moment he realizes what I'm about to say, as bewilderment gives way to hurt. "But I don't love you, Spencer, and it's wrong of me to lead you on any longer. You deserve someone to give you the world and then some, but sadly, that someone isn't me."

To his credit, he doesn't rant. He doesn't accuse me of dragging out our relationship because it suited me. He doesn't yell that I used him. He doesn't say anything. But I see the devastation our break up has caused when he turns away, his back ramrod straight, before glancing over his shoulder, the depth of his pain piercing me to my core.

"You do what you want, Cora. You always have," he says, his tone frigid. "But I'm not leaving, because this is the only home I've ever known, the only place I've ever belonged, and I'm not giving that up, no matter how much you want me to."

"You don't have to leave..." I trail off as he stalks out the door and slams it on his way out.

CHAPTER 31
LUCY

My legs are rubbery as I sprint up the corridor past too many empty rooms. Craig and Demi's room is at the opposite end to mine and I fall against their door and pound on it, too afraid to glance over my shoulder in case whatever is haunting my room has followed me. But at least that infernal moaning and pleas for help have stopped, though it has done little to calm my erratic heartbeat.

I continue banging at the door and when Craig opens it, I'm instantly relieved and embarrassed. He's staring at me like I've lost my mind and I don't blame him. He must think I'm crazy, pounding at his door in the middle of the night. I have no idea what time it is, but by his spiked hair and droopy eyes, he was fast asleep.

"Lucy? Is everything alright?"

I refrain from stating the obvious, that I wouldn't be a quivering mess trying to break down his door during the night if I was fine.

"Sorry to wake you. But my room... I saw... and heard..." I'm stumbling over my words, but what can I say? That an inexplicable force possessing my room is trying to drive me mad with visions and pleas for help?

"Did you have a nightmare?"

I wish. Nightmares are banished as soon as you wake. What I saw and heard only started after I woke.

"I don't know," I murmur, embarrassment flushing my cheeks. "I keep hearing and seeing things, but I'm not asleep."

His eyes are wide, his brows almost reaching his hairline. "This place is creepy, and I'm sorry if I freaked you out the other day by saying it feels like we're being watched. You probably had a doozy of a nightmare and it resonated when you woke?"

Craig's reaching for a logical explanation when there is none. Believe me, I've tried. In all my twenty-five years, I've never had a psychic experience. I felt nothing when I went on a ghost tour through Manhattan with other librarians. I love reading paranormal and horror, the creepier the better. But what's happening to me here? It's inexplicable.

"Lucy?" Demi appears by Craig's side, sleep-tousled and rubbing her eyes. "What's wrong?"

I want to say 'everything' but I'm feeling increasingly foolish standing here in my pajamas, trying to explain what's been happening to me since I set foot in Arcania.

"I'm okay," I mumble, thankful that I've stopped shaking, but knowing I'll have to head back to my room shortly and not looking forward to it one bit.

"Do you want to come in?" Demi nudges Craig with her elbow but he's not budging. I don't blame him for not wanting to let the crazy woman into their room.

Before I can answer, Craig says, "It's four thirty, Luce. Perhaps it's best you head back to your room and try to get some more sleep?"

I almost laugh at Demi's side-eye at her husband, but he's right. I can't depend on strangers. I'd been too petrified earlier to think clearly and my flight reaction had overpowered my fight. Maybe if I confronted whatever is haunting me, it'll stop. That's one of the things the guide on the ghost tour had said: a ghost wants to be acknowledged and once you do that firmly, it'll stop bothering you. I can live in hope.

But the visions I'm seeing aren't ghostly. They're totally random: robed people, the compass, Mom. The latter is most disconcerting of all. It's not Mom as I knew her, but my mother as a teen.

In looking for answers, is Mom trying to tell me something? If so, she appears terrified every time I've seen her, so perhaps she's telling me to get the hell out of here. I won't need much encouragement to do that. After tonight, I think I'm done.

"Lucy?" Demi's voice is filled with concern and I refocus on these kind people who I've woken with my freak out.

"I'm okay. Sorry to wake you. I'll confront the ghosts next time rather than fleeing."

They're staring at me like I'm out of my mind, and I turn away and stride quickly down the corridor back to my room. I may not understand what's going on, but I know one thing.

I won't be sleeping for the rest of the night.

CHAPTER 32
CORA

T HEN

FOR TWENTY-FIVE YEARS, I try to immerse myself in Arcania. I renovate, keeping the integrity of the original mansion but adding modern rooms onto the back. A new kitchen, a dazzling dining room, a gym, a yoga studio and later, when I transform it into a wellness retreat, a day spa.

My B&B idea never really took off because of those pesky rumors—turns out, most people looking to vacation research their proposed house choice and discover how Harlan and Ava died, the implication some workers disappear, and assume Arcania is cursed. The police interrogated me in the early days, when a family reported their son missing, and Arcania had been his last place of employment.

But what could I tell them? I didn't have any proof Harlan had got rid of those employees who suddenly vanished and with the house bracketed by the swamp and the sea, what could they do? A search would be futile.

Besides, Harlan had picked his marks carefully. Most of those missing workers had been runaways like me, so nobody would miss them. And with the runaways not in contact with family, they could've vanished anywhere. The only reason that family had reported their son missing was he'd had a change of heart and sent them a postcard from Nag's Head and the police had followed his trail to here.

With my bed-and-breakfast idea stalled before it began, I pondered what else I could do with my newly renovated mansion so that I wouldn't be so alone. I wanted to fill it with people; I desperately needed the distraction. That same night, I watched a documentary on wellness retreats in Australia and I knew Arcania could provide something similar here.

But I needed a hook, something to distinguish Arcania from other similar places, and came up with the digital detox angle. The rest is history. It's amazing how many people want to go off grid. I have repeat customers who come annually for a week of good food—Daphne's skills in the kitchen have improved exponentially over the years—beach walks, and general relaxation.

In all this transformation, Spencer is my right-hand man. Surprisingly, he didn't leave when I ended our relationship. Seems his love for Arcania matches mine. We're good friends, but I'm watchful for any signs he's sticking around because he still has feelings for me. But I've seen nothing in the last two decades, so I believe him when he says Arcania is the only home he's ever known and that's why he'll never leave.

It's strange though. If he loves this place as much as I do, why isn't he more invested in the legend?

Shocking, I know, that I too have succumbed to the lure of the gold compass. Not that I believe all that stuff about it appeasing angry Viking gods, but finding it will put Arcania on the map. We'll be the most famous wellness retreat in the world and guests will flock.

I now employ divers regularly to scour the shipwreck, but so far, nothing. Spencer continues to dive also, but it's nowhere near the wreckage. I know, because I accompany him. Not into the water—my fear of the ocean hasn't subsided over the years—but in the boat. I like the wind on my face. It clears my head. And when I'm alone in the boat while he dives, I can focus on Arcania, a speck in the distance, and be thankful something so magnificent is mine.

Being out on the ocean also banishes the doubts that creep in. Because strange things still happen at night within Arcania's walls. I wake in a cold sweat with a heaviness on my chest, like someone's sitting there. Even on a still night, I can hear creaks and groans. I see visions of Harlan, enraged and coming for me with arms outstretched, like he wants to strangle me.

I dismiss these oddities as figments of my imagination, a residual guilt for how I killed my husband. So being out on the water, with the wind at my back and the vision of Arcania at my front, ground me.

Spencer and I had an early start this morning because we're fully booked, with twelve new guests arriving today and fourteen tomorrow. We're at capacity for the next two weeks and ensuring every guest has a good time might mean repeat business, which we thrive on.

Once they're all checked in by late afternoon, I need to go over tonight's menu with Daphne. But as I'm making my way to the kitchen, I'm waylaid by Raylene, a sixty-something Wall Street banker whose husband insisted she take a week off from being glued to her cell.

"Excuse me, Cora," she calls out, and when I turn, she stops and stares at me so intently I wonder if I have a smudge on my nose.

"What can I help you with, Raylene?"

"Uh..." She blinks and gives me a rueful smile. "For a minute there, you look exactly like someone I know."

"We all have a doppelgänger somewhere in the world, apparently."

"So I've heard." Her scrutiny is slightly unnerving. "Well, if you ever want to see yours, go to the Lower Manhattan Library. One of the librarians there could be your double."

"I'll keep that in mind. Now, did you want something?"

Raylene's smile is rueful. "Actually, yes. I've taken a week off work to come here, but there's a conference I'm attending in a month and I may need to confirm my accommodations. Do you think I could have access to my cell to do that?"

I stifle a grin. This isn't the first time a workaholic has used a flimsy excuse to gain access to a screen.

Schooling my face into an impassive mask, I shake my head. "I'm sorry, Raylene. That's against the rules. You'll get your cell back when you check out."

She frowns. "I can't believe I agreed to this."

I want to quote the benefits of a week off from screen time, but she won't appreciate it. Or worse, I'll alienate a guest on the first day. So I settle for a placating smile and she shrugs and walks away.

That would've been the end of it, if I hadn't glanced at Ava's portrait on my right. I'd had it painted by a local artist two years after her death, from a photo we'd taken on the beach, and not a day goes by that I don't stare at it with heaviness in my heart.

In the photo, we'd been standing so close our heads are touching and I remember Harlan saying we could be twins at the time. With only eighteen years separating us, we could've passed for sisters, and with Raylene's talk of my lookalike, I stare closer at the portrait, unable to subdue the faintest doubt.

Is Ava still alive?

It's something I've pondered over the years. A hope that perhaps my clever daughter faked her death in order to escape Arcania. I'd even hired a private investigator nine months after she vanished in that swamp, but he'd come up with nothing.

It's lunacy to even ponder the librarian that Raylene mentioned could be my Ava, but I know myself. I'll obsess over this. I'll create fanciful scenarios in my head or a fictional reunion. I'll ruminate at length when I should be focusing on Arcania.

Nothing will appease my curiosity.

Except a trip to that Manhattan library.

CHAPTER 33
LUCY

After my hellish night, I'm relieved to find the breakfast room empty. I help myself to a croissant and orange juice, wanting to eat quickly so I can ask Cora about the early check-out policy. I'm assuming I'll lose the rest of my pre-payment and won't get a refund but I don't care. Searching for answers here has proved fruitless and I can't spend another night being spooked.

Nothing happened after I returned to my room in the wee small hours. But that's because I switched on every light and didn't sleep, which proves the darkness brings this house to life and I don't want to tempt fate again.

I finish my juice when Jase and Cindy stroll into the dining room. They're wearing matching gray sweatpants and white T-shirts, their arms locked around each other's waists, and her head is resting on his shoulder. Second honeymoon indeed.

"Hey." I raise my hand in greeting and they smile at me in unison.

"Good morning," Jase says, echoed by Cindy. "Jeez, this place is quiet."

"Yeah," Cindy says, disengaging from her husband to select a bowl of oatmeal and a blueberry muffin from the sideboard. "It's just the three of us now."

The glass I'm holding almost slips from my hand and I carefully place it on the table in front of me. "What happened to Craig and Demi?"

"Checked out early," Jase says, before cramming an apricot into his mouth.

"We saw them leave at dawn," Cindy adds, her nose crinkling. "So weird, to cut the week short and head out so early."

"Probably couldn't stand being offline for seven days, especially if they're influencers." Jase rolls his eyes. "Though I don't know why you'd come here, knowing it's to digitally detox, and then quit early because you have no willpower."

Cindy lays a hand on his forearm. "They could've left for any reason, honey."

Yeah, like escaping a madwoman who almost broke down their door in the middle of the night.

Jase gently bumps Cindy with his shoulder. "Don't you think it's weird, Lucy? Rushing off like that?"

"It does seem odd," I say, knowing I won't be far behind.

With Craig and Demi gone, my room at the end of the long corridor is the only one occupied and I can't face another night like the one I just had with no one nearby.

"You two are conspiracy theorists." Cindy chuckles. "That's the thing about places like this. You don't know who your fellow guests are. You meet fleetingly, then never see each other again. But for those few days you're here, you're almost closer than family."

Jase rolls his eyes again. "We've barely made it out of

155

our room, babe, so Craig and Demi could've been vampires for all we know."

I stiffen and Jase laughs. "Don't you think this place could house a vampire or two, Lucy? It's definitely got a haunted vibe in the original house." He waves his arm around. "Not here, though. You would've thought they would've renovated the entire place when they modernized this part."

"I think it's charming," Cindy says, but I notice her rubbing her arms like she's trying to stave off goosebumps.

"Is your room modern?" I should've asked this before, to see if I'm the only one with potential ghosts.

Jase shakes his head. "We're in the opposite wing to you, and while the bathroom has been renovated, the room is a tad gloomy."

If I knew them better, I'd ask if anything weird has happened in their room but I've potentially scared off one couple, I don't want to do it again, because the last thing I want is to be left alone here before I've checked out.

"Honestly? If I wasn't with Jase, I'd be a little scared." A hint of fear lurks in Cindy's eyes. "The place is nothing like what I expected. I mean, I like the newer areas, like the rec rooms and here, but the original house could feature in a horror film."

Jase slings an arm across Cindy's shoulders. "Babe, Lucy is here alone and you're freaking her out."

To the contrary, I'm glad I'm not the only one who gets creepy vibes from Arcania's original mansion.

Cindy grimaces. "Sorry, Lucy."

"No worries," I say, but it's a lie. Because my biggest worry is leaving here without the answers I came for, but I'm in self-preservation mode after last night and the sooner I see Cora to check out, the better.

I stand. "Enjoy your breakfast."

I hear Jase's loud whisper, "You scared her off," but Cindy's response is muffled as I reach the door and almost run into the woman I want to see.

Has Cora been eavesdropping?

"Good morning, dear. Sleep well?"

Cora's expression is benign, but I can't shake the impression that her eyes are hiding a world of secrets.

"Not really, and that's what I want to talk to you about."

"Is there something wrong with your room? Because we can change it."

I shake my head. "That won't be necessary."

Her eyebrows rise at my curt tone. "Let's discuss this in my office."

It's a short stroll from the dining room to the main foyer, and Jase is right. The contrast between the back of the property and the original mansion is stark. The gloom is instant as we step into the foyer, like a shroud covering everything, and I suppress a shudder. The dark velvet furniture, the Viking ancestral paintings, the sconces, all accentuate that what happened in my room last night wasn't a result of sleeplessness, grief or a wild imagination.

Something is wrong with this house, and it's not happy with me.

If Mom stayed here at some stage, I'm not surprised she fled. But what was so bad that after fleeing here, it made her into a recluse? Unless she already had agoraphobia while living here, though I can't see anyone wanting to be confined here and never going out.

"Actually, I wanted to talk to you." Cora opens her office door and gestures me in. "Your questions yesterday got me thinking. I'm considering hiring a ghostwriter to document the history of Arcania, and your interest made me think you'd be the perfect candidate to help research."

I'm stunned by her offer. It's the perfect opportunity to discover more about Mom's ties to this place and gives me a legitimate excuse to poke around.

But I'm uneasy. Why now? She'd blown up at me yesterday for my curiosity. Today she wants me to delve into the history of this place.

Something isn't right and the hairs on the back of my neck snap to attention when she closes the door.

I don't like being alone with her.

"That's an interesting offer," I say, choosing my words carefully so not to antagonize her. "But I was actually wanting to check out today."

"You too?" She sighs and sinks into the worn leather chair behind her desk. "Did something happen last night I'm not aware of?"

Yeah, your freaky-ass mansion is haunted and somehow the spirits are focused on me.

I settle for saying, "I was surprised to hear Craig and Demi checked out too."

"They cited work commitments in the note they left with their key, but who rushes off like that before the sun is barely over the horizon?" She tsk-tsks. "Are you sure something didn't happen last night?"

Cora is the last person I'd confide in and I need to distract her. "I'm flattered by your offer to research the history of Arcania, but wouldn't someone local be more fitting for the job?"

"This is a passion project for me and it requires someone with genuine interest." Her eyes glitter with enthusiasm. "You seem fascinated with the history by the questions you were asking me and I apologize for flying off the handle. We've had people staying over the years who want to disparage what we do here and I can't be too careful, so your questions triggered me."

Interesting. Why would anyone asking about the history of Arcania trigger her unless there's something to hide?

I hate to admit I'm curious. "How long would this project take?"

"I thought you could start your research in person here, then when you get home, you could continue online." Her shoulders slump. "I'm not sure how long it will take me to find a good ghostwriter, so whatever factual information you can find ahead of time will be an excellent incentive for someone to take this on."

Okay, so she's not wanting me to stay beyond the week I already booked, which is good. I'm not sure I'll last the next few nights, let alone any longer. And despite her offer sounding genuine, I can't shake the feeling she's not to be trusted.

"Who has access to the guest rooms?"

My question comes out of left field and is designed to test her. She appears genuinely startled, her eyebrows shooting high. "There are two master keys. One in the kitchen, which Daphne and Spencer can access if needed, and one here." She points to a metal filing cabinet behind her. "It's always locked. Why do you ask?"

"Because someone placed a diving suit in my room yesterday and when I woke later, it was gone."

She pales and grips the edge of the desk so tightly her knuckles pop. "Are you sure?"

"Yes," I snap, and she flinches. I already think I'm going crazy; I don't need her to reiterate it.

"I'll ask Daphne about it, but it's highly doubtful she

would do such a thing." Her brows draw together in consternation and I wonder if she's faking it, because I want to ask, "would you?"

"So what do you say to my offer?" The corners of her mouth ease upward into a smile. "I think you'll be perfect."

That makes one of us, because I can't quell the persistent doubts that this house isn't good for me.

CHAPTER 34
CORA

T HEN

W‍ITH A‍RCANIA HEAVILY BOOKED, it's another two weeks before I can sneak off to New York City. I tell Daphne and Spencer I'm checking out the newest competition on Long Island, because I know Spencer will interrogate me if he discovers I'm off to the city.

He's odd that way. Whenever I leave Arcania—which has happened a grand total of three times in the last twenty-five years—he asks me where I'm going and for how long, like he's afraid I'll leave and not return. It's sweet in a way but telling him I'm off on a crazy hunch is a far cry from those other times I left: for Mom's funeral—I finally reached out to her after a decade here and we reestablished tenuous contact—for a few days in Arizona at a renowned health spa on a reconnaissance mission, and for a uterine procedure when the walls thickened around menopause.

New York City is teeming as usual and as I'm jostled on the sidewalks, I crave the sanctuary of Arcania more than ever. This expedition is beyond foolish and as I enter the small library, I'm holding my breath.

"Ridiculous," I mutter as I stroll past the carrels and scan the front desk for my supposed double.

But I only see an older woman—Gladys, according to her name tag—and no other librarians in sight. I spend two hours pretending to scour shelves, from biographies to science fiction, mysteries to romance, self-help to thrillers. Gladys approaches me once to offer assistance, and I wave her off. I could ask if other librarians are working today, but that'll be plain weird.

Besides, if my daughter faked her disappearance, why hasn't she contacted me in all these years? She may have been terrified of her father, but what did I do? It's bugged me every time I've contemplated the possibility of her being alive, so tipping her off that someone is asking for her won't help my cause. I'll just come back tomorrow.

But as I make my way toward the entrance, a door opens to my left, next to rooms marked 'Student Study' and a woman backs out, pulling a trolley laden with books.

"Gladys, I've finished culling the women's fiction section, and here's what I'll put back on the shelves," the woman says, and Gladys says, "Thanks, Lucy."

I pause, and as she turns, my lungs seize.

Lucy isn't my daughter.

But she looks so much like Ava she has to be my granddaughter.

And that means Ava is alive.

And my only child, who I sacrificed everything for in order to protect her has deceived me for the last twenty-six years.

CHAPTER 35

LUCY

After leaving Cora's office, I decide to take a walk on the beach to clear my head. I'm seriously considering accepting Cora's offer to research Arcania when I should be packing instead.

Am I tempting fate by staying here until the end of the week?

Any sane person would run a mile after what happened last night, not to mention all the other weird stuff that's been going on. And I can't imagine sleeping in that room again.

But what if I don't have to? Researching the history of the wellness retreat will give me carte blanche to other rooms, the grounds, the tunnels...It's a perfect cover to find answers about Mom, yet I can't shake the feeling that it's too good to be true.

I'd been right to question Cora about hiring someone local rather than me. Someone older who may have connections to Arcania in the past. Though I had been questioning her and it may be a simple case of being in the right place at the right time.

I never used to be this skeptical, but discovering Mom had hidden a side of her from me has made me question everything.

I follow a winding path down to the beach and when I hit the sand, I slip off my sneakers. There's no one on the beach bar a distant figure that's approaching at a rapid pace; a jogger. I trudge toward the water's edge, close enough to feel the sea spray on my face, but far enough away the ocean can't touch me.

Did Mom once frolic in these waves despite her fear of water? Did she roam this shoreline in search of shells? Did she stare out to sea, wishing she could escape? Countless questions I'll never know the answer to and if I stay, maybe I would?

As the jogger nears me, I see it's Spencer. He's running like he has a dozen demons on his tail and is waving his arms at me as if he's guiding a jet pilot onto a carrier.

"Spencer, hey. You're back—"

"You have... to leave..." He's gasping for air, his hands braced above his knees as he drags in deep breaths.

Not this again. What is it with this guy and his constant warnings?

"Spencer, unless you give me a legitimate reason why you think I should leave Arcania, I'm not listening to any more of your senseless warnings."

He coughs, violent heaves that shake his chest, before he slowly straightens. I know I'm not going to like what he has to say by his somber expression.

"You have to leave because Cora killed your mother and you may be next."

CHAPTER 36
CORA

T HEN

I WATCH Lucy push her book trolley toward the last shelf. Despite the urge to run after her, grab her, and ask what the hell is going on, I don't move. I can't. My feet are rooted to the floor as I ponder the implications of discovering the daughter I loved more than life itself faked her own death to get away from me.

That's the kicker in all this.

Why did Ava run when she didn't have to?

I ran away from my mother because she didn't have a maternal bone in her body and I bore the brunt of that when she couldn't see what was right in front of her face: her sleazy boyfriends coming onto me. I wanted her protection, or at least the knowledge that I could trust her enough to go to her if things got really bad.

I got nothing. So I left and didn't look back. I married a

man wrong for me in a blatant attempt for security, to protect my daughter in a way my mother hadn't protected me, and I'd stuck with him for fear I'd end up alone and poor.

But I'm not my mother. I never made Ava feel unsupported. I would've done anything to protect her and her unborn child, and I had. I'd killed Harlan for her. It may have been a rash, impulsive decision born of rage, but I'd done it for my baby.

And how did she repay me?

By running away.

By letting me grieve.

By letting the pain of loss fester until it consumed me.

Anger prickles my skin and I turn away before I do something silly. Confronting Lucy when it's her mother I want to see will be foolhardy. I need to bide my time and plan what I'm going to say when I see Ava.

I cross the street and enter a cafe, order a coffee with cream, and take a seat by the window. It gives me an unimpeded view of the library so I can see when Lucy leaves. It's almost five and I don't have to wait long. Twenty minutes later, Lucy exits the library. Only then do I realize I haven't touched my coffee, I've been so focused on not missing her.

I stand so abruptly coffee sloshes on the table, but I don't wait. I bolt out the door in time to see her turn a corner. I break into a jog. She's half a block ahead of me and I slow to a walk as passersby cast me concerned glances.

Adrenaline courses through me, making my heart pound despite my sedate pace now and my fingers tingle. I follow her for six blocks before she slows in front of a modest brownstone. It's tiny but well kept, with a terra-cotta pot filled with petunias beside the front door.

Lucy's rummaging in her bag, probably in search of

keys, when the front door opens. Only a smidgeon, but it's enough.

I see my daughter for the first time in over two decades.

I'm behind a tree so she has no hope of seeing me and I lean against it, grateful for the support. The bark scratches my cheek, my face is pressed so hard against it. I close my eyes against the burn of tears and when I reopen them, the door is closed.

The urge to run across the road and confront Ava is strong, but I can't think right now, let alone formulate words.

What can I say? That I love her despite what she put me through? That I hate her for abandoning me and depriving me of a granddaughter? That she's as selfish as her father for hurting me, the one person on her side?

That's when the tears start to fall. Not a trickle, but a torrent, and I'm sobbing so hard I can't breathe.

No, she can't see me like this. I need to regroup. Calm down. Figure out what I'm going to say. I'll check into a hotel for the night and come back tomorrow.

Time enough to confront my daughter then and get what she owed me.

Answers.

CHAPTER 37
LUCY

I stare at Spencer in disbelief. Is everything and everyone in this place possessed?

"What are you talking about? My mother got hit by a bus."

His gaze is pitying. "And I suspect Cora pushed her in front of it."

"You're out of your mind." I take a step back from him, another. The man is unhinged. He's right about one thing. No matter how tempting Cora's offer is, I need to follow my gut and get the hell out of here.

"Just hear me out." He holds out his hands, palms up, like he's got nothing to hide. He'd be one of the few around here. "What I'm about to tell you may sound unbelievable, but I want you to keep an open mind, okay?"

I won't make a promise I can't keep, but I manage a terse nod for him to continue.

"I recognized you the moment you arrived." He pinches the bridge of his nose and takes a few deep breaths, as if he's having trouble continuing.

"I don't know you, so you mean I remind you of someone?"

"You're the spitting image of Ava," he murmurs, sadness clouding his eyes. "You had to be her daughter."

"So you weren't just messing with me when you said I was just like her and you actually knew my mother?"

His nod is brief as he glances away, his gaze fixed on the ocean while a myriad of emotions play across his face: pain, loss, regret, sadness. I can't fathom it, but it gives me hope that this man is telling the truth and he can provide me with insight into her time here.

"Why didn't you say something sooner? You hinted at it, saying I'm just like her, but then you vanished before I could ask more."

He drags his gaze back to me. "It was wrong of me to say that because I hoped you wouldn't stay. That you'd leave and I wouldn't have to tell you the truth."

"The only reason I came here is to discover the truth, so please, whatever you have to say, I want to hear it."

His brow creases. "It will put you in grave danger. Which is why your mother fled in the first place, to protect you."

Spencer is talking in riddles, but with each proclamation, I know I'm one step closer to solving the puzzle of Mom's links to Arcania.

"So my mother spent some time here?" I hesitate, unsure whether to trust him but needing to join the dots. "After she died, I discovered the *vegvisir* tattooed on the sole of her foot. I'd never seen it before and it shocked me. When I looked it up online, I discovered it's the logo for Arcania and that's why I booked a week here, to find out how my mom is linked to this place."

"They made us all get tattooed," Spencer whispers, his words whipped away by the wind. "Branded."

A shiver runs down my spine. "Who made you?"

"Magnus and Helga Medville. They opened the doors of Arcania to anyone who needed a place to stay and a job on the pretext of organic farming. But what they really wanted was a bunch of minions willing to do their bidding." Bitterness brackets his mouth. "They ran this place like a cult, complete with charismatic leaders and clueless followers."

I hate the thought of Mom being brainwashed and trapped here to the extent she had to run so far and hide away. "My mom was a follower?"

Spencer takes an eternity to answer and when he does, his somber expression alerts me to the fact I won't like what he has to say.

"No, your mother was the daughter of one of the leaders."

He pauses and I swear my heart stops when he says, "Ava was Cora's daughter."

CHAPTER 38
CORA

T HEN

I FORMULATE A PLAN.

If Ava's gone to such great lengths to hide all these years, if I show up on her doorstep, she won't let me in. I don't want to give her a chance to slam the door in my face so the only option is to meet elsewhere.

Not a test to see if she wants to meet me after all this time per se, but somewhere impartial, surrounded by people, so she can see I'm not mad at her. Even though I am. A lot. But I doused my anger with tiny bottles of whiskey and vodka from the minibar last night and while I'm not completely over it, I know I have to play this cool or risk losing my daughter for good.

It's a weird feeling, vacillating between hope and fury, love, and regret. I hadn't slept a wink all night despite the comfy bed—I'd checked the mattress brand because guests at Arcania will love sleeping on clouds, which is exactly what it felt like last night—because I couldn't stop the questions pinging through my head.

Did Ava leave because of me?

Did I do something?

Did she love me at all?

Did she not respect me for staying with Harlan all those years?

Did she blame me for not protecting her from Harlan more?

Or the doozy, did Spencer say something to imply he was her father, and she hates me for lying to her?

It went on and on all night until I rose at dawn, showered, and packed my overnight bag. I won't be coming back to this hotel. By tonight, I'll either be staying with my daughter and granddaughter, or on a flight back home. Because if Ava wants nothing to do with me, I will not stay in the city in the vain hope of convincing her to change her mind.

Either she comes clean about everything and welcomes me back into her life, or I'm out of here.

It won't be easy walking away, but I'll steel myself. She's hurt me enough by perpetuating the myth of an alligator taking her. She gutted me. No mother should ever have to live through losing a child and I'm going to use that, appeal to her maternal side, make her question how she'd feel if she lost Lucy.

I'm standing opposite her house by seven a.m. my stomach growling. I haven't eaten since lunch yesterday but I can't face food, not when I'm likely to regurgitate the lot depending on what happens in the next hour.

I wait until Lucy leaves, and the way Ava peeks through the half-open door, fearful and suspicious, before slamming it on Lucy's back tells me I'm doing the right thing in giving her the option to meet elsewhere.

When Lucy is out of sight, I sprint across the road and shove my note under the door, give a quick knock, before running back to my hiding place on the off-chance Ava opens the door to see who left it.

She doesn't, and I glance at my watch. I've given her forty-five minutes to shower and dress if she needs to and meet me at a hotdog stand near Central Park.

I wonder if she gets the significance. We'd been watching a movie once—I can't remember the name—when she was about ten, and she'd never had a hot dog, what with Harlan's obsession with organic produce, so when she'd seen the stand outside Central Park she'd announced when she was older she'd spend all day at the stand and consume as many hotdogs as humanly possible. I'd laughed and cuddled her, saying we'd make it a contest.

It never happened. Neither of us left Arcania under Harlan's watchful eye and I wonder how many other dreams my daughter harbored and never shared because she knew they wouldn't come true.

Regret churns my gut as I stroll to our meeting place. I wonder if others rehash the past in their head as often as I do, envisaging different outcomes. If I hadn't accepted Harlan's offer to work at Arcania when I first ran away, would I still be rich now? Would I have clawed my way to the top some other way or would I be destitute, getting by on odd jobs, scrimping and saving, never having enough?

Would Ava still be with me if I'd accepted Spencer's initial offer to leave Arcania with him? Would we be a happy family, content with little financially but close? Would I have had more children?

I'd made sure that didn't happen with Harlan, my

meticulous birth control methods bordering on an obsession. Thankfully, he'd lost interest in me as his passion for making Arcania great grew, but I never trusted him not to impregnate me for another heir. Lucky for me, he was satisfied having a girl inherit Arcania in the future.

I hate mulling over a bunch of 'what ifs', but I can't help it. My life could've been so different if I hadn't chosen security for Ava and, in doing so, marrying a monster.

And how had my daughter repaid me? By abandoning me. By deceiving me. By robbing me of the only family I have.

I'm so deep in my musings I almost miss Ava as she passes me. She's dressed in all black, from her lace-up ankle boots to the beanie pulled low over her ears, but I'd recognize her anywhere. My daughter has a distinctive walk, longer strides than others, just like her father. I always thought Spencer would go places with those strides. Instead, he's curtailed them to stay with me. Yet another thing to feel guilty about.

Not that I asked him to. I made it more than clear, but I'd be lying if I didn't admit that a small part of me likes his loyalty, that he makes me feel safe, like I always have someone watching over me.

It's Ava's walk that does it. The familiarity of it; of her. I can't follow her all the way to the hot dog stand. I need to confront her now.

"Ava," I call out, and she stops, her fingers curling into fists, instantly defensive.

She must recognize my voice because when she turns, her expression is part joy, part fear.

I scan her face, taking in the new lines around her eyes, the grooves alongside her mouth. But her skin is clear and at forty-three, she looks a decade younger.

I want to run to her, to sweep her into my arms, to hug her close and never let go, but my feet won't move. I'm trembling, the shock of seeing my beloved daughter again after all this time, the reality that she's alive, is overwhelming.

"Ava..." It's a whisper this time and I clear my throat, wanting to say so much to my daughter but unsure where to start.

"How did you find me, Mom?"

Not exactly what I imagined her first words to me in decades would be and my elation at finding her alive fades, replaced by the anger I subdued last night.

"Does it matter how I found you, considering I've been under the misapprehension you've been dead for twenty-six years?"

"I'm sorry."

She shrugs, like what she's put me through means nothing, and I lose it.

"Is that all you've got to say? I've been to hell and back, Ava, and for what? What did I ever do to you?"

I'm yelling and early morning commuters hurry past us, heads down, not wanting to engage with the crazy woman.

"It's what you didn't do that was the problem, Mom." Tears fill her eyes, but she lifts her chin, defiant. "You didn't stand up for me against Dad. When I wanted to go to school like normal kids, when I wanted to go to college, you just stood there and said nothing. When I wanted to go on vacation and he refused, you stood by him." She snorts. "And I get it. You were afraid of him, too. But we could've escaped, you and me, together. Instead, you watched him force me to get that stupid tattoo on my eighteenth birthday, and I knew then I could never rely on you. It was the final straw for me."

Her upper lip curls in a sneer as her truths stab at me deeper than knives. "I knew when I got pregnant that if he found out he'd make me abort and you'd do nothing to support me, so I left before you let me down yet again. Because there's no way in hell I would've given up on my baby like you gave up on me."

Guilt that every word she's uttered is correct chokes me, but I manage to say, "How did you escape?"

She waves away my question. "Irrelevant now. You need to leave, Mom, and never come back." She gnaws on her bottom lip in a gesture so familiar I start to cry. "You've been dead to me a long time. Let's keep it that way."

My heart is splintering into a million pieces as she walks away but I can't let it end like this. If she hears my side, she'll forgive me. She has to.

She's about to cross a busy road when I reach her.

"Ava, please, you have to listen to me. Give me a chance to explain. I miss you. I love you."

She doesn't hear me above the traffic noise so I grab her arm. She startles and glances over her shoulder, and as she sees who's accosted her, she yanks her arm out of my hand.

But in doing so, she staggers back a little, loses her footing on the curb, and falls.

Into the path of an oncoming bus.

CHAPTER 39
LUCY

I gape at Spencer, unable to process the truth.

"But if Mom is Cora's daughter, that makes me her granddaughter..." I shake my head, unable to comprehend the enormity of this. Nothing makes sense. "Cora's Ava died. Daphne said they found a finger in the swamp. Unless my outlandish suspicion is right and Mom faked her death to escape this place for whatever reason."

Spencer's sorrow is palpable, radiating off him in waves that make his shoulders slump and his back bow. "I planted that finger. I found a body washed up ashore about five miles from here on my daily walk and before I called the police, I..." he clears his throat. "Severed the finger because I knew it was Ava's way out. A rash, impulsive decision I'll never regret."

My head is spinning and my knees are shaking so hard I sink to the sand and wrap my arms around them. "You helped my mother escape."

It's a statement, not a question, because I can see Spencer is genuine. He's hurting, and that means he must've cared for my mom enough to help her flee Arcania.

"I did. I helped her because she'd only just discovered she was pregnant with you and she knew she had to get out."

"Why?"

He grimaces and waves his arm in the direction of the mansion on the cliffs that's not visible from here. "Because she didn't want you raised at Arcania. To go through what she had. To become one of Cora's underlings."

My chest aches with the enormity of what Spencer has revealed.

Mom fled Arcania to protect me.

So how bad must it have been for her growing up here?

"If it's so awful, why did you stay?"

He drags in a breath and blows it out slowly, before sinking to the sand beside me. "In case you came here one day looking for answers."

He eyeballs me and I can't fathom the tears in his eyes. "That's why I've been warning you to leave from the start because I recognized you instantly because of your similarities to Ava, and if I did, Cora may too. Has she said anything?"

I shake my head, disconcerted by the idea Cora may know who I am and is toying with me regardless.

"It doesn't mean she doesn't suspect." His jaw tightens. "Has anything weird happened to you since I've been away?"

I want to tell him about the visions, the voices, the diving suit. But can I fully trust him? For all I know, he could be fishing for information and will run to Cora and tell her. Because if my supposed grandmother is that bad, he would've left years ago too. To hear him say he stuck around in case I visited is ludicrous.

"Tell me, Lucy. What's been going on?"

"I'm not buying the fact you stayed all these years on the odd chance I would show up one day. What's the real reason?"

His gaze slides away as his fingers pluck at his frayed sleeve. He's nervous, which means he's hiding something.

"Spencer, I want to hear why you think Cora had something to do with Mom's death, but I'll be honest and say I'm not sure if I believe a word coming out of your mouth. So tell me why you thought I'd show up here one day."

He drags his eyes back to meet mine, pain shimmering in their depths.

"Because Ava was my daughter and you're my granddaughter."

I'm shell-shocked for the second time in as many minutes and press my fingertips to my temples. It does little to ease the tension making my head ache.

This is ludicrous, and I have no idea whether to believe him or not.

"Are you and Cora involved?"

He shakes his head. "Not anymore. Cora was eighteen when she first arrived here and we hit it off immediately. We hung out a lot. Then one night..." He reddens and looks away. "I pictured us leaving Arcania together. But Cora was drawn to Harlan Medville too and the next thing I knew they were engaged and she was pregnant."

"Did you question the paternity?"

He nods, his expression so bleak I wish I could comfort him. "She assured me the baby was Harlan's and Ava was born a few weeks early, so I had to accept the truth. But as Ava grew in that first year, I'd find myself studying her, and seeing snippets of myself in her." He grimaces. "It may have been wishful thinking but I couldn't take the chance of leaving in case Cora had lied to me. I'd already witnessed strange occurrences here, the cult-like atmosphere, so I stayed so I could watch over her child." His intake of breath is sharp. "My child. I knew I couldn't leave. I'd do anything I could to protect her."

His eyes glaze over, lost in remembrance. "We bonded from the start, almost like Ava had a sixth sense I was someone special to her. She trusted me when she didn't trust many in Arcania, not even her mother. Which ended up being a smart thing to do."

He blinks rapidly, and I hope he's not going to cry. "Cora wanted to bind Ava to Arcania. To ensure she had an heir to carry on after she dies. That tattoo on your mother's sole? Cora stood by and watched as Harlan had her daughter branded like the rest of his workers in some warped way to prove loyalty. We all have them. And when you don't want them, like Ava didn't, it's degrading."

I press my hand to my chest. It does nothing to ease the tightness making breathing difficult. "What about my father?"

"He was a nice boy. A year older than Ava, a backpacker from California passing through. He was a carpenter who did some renovations for a while, then stayed on to work the orchard for a few months because he was smitten with Ava, and the feeling was mutual. Unfortunately, Harlan noticed too, and he started keeping an obsessive watch over Ava. Then Sam disappeared. We were told he'd left to continue his travels, but he would've never left Ava without saying goodbye."

Disapproval pinches his mouth. "Ava found out she was pregnant two weeks later and confided in me because she suspected what I thought, that Harlan had made Sam disappear and Cora probably knew about it, either by offering him a large sum of money to leave or..."

Spencer doesn't need to finish the sentence. The implication is clear, and I hug my knees tighter to my chest.

"I promised I'd help her escape. Her only thought was to protect her unborn child. Being taken by an alligator in the swamp seemed the most likely, but I knew Cora wouldn't buy it unless there was some kind of proof. So when I saw that body on the beach...it was gruesome, but I had to get that finger."

I wince, though somewhat impressed at Spencer mutilating a dead body to help save his daughter. "But how did she get away if Cora was watching her?"

"The tunnels. I know them like the back of my hand and one of them ends about two miles away and at low tide, it's easy. I'd been diving for years, feigning an interest in finding Cora's special golden compass, never telling her I found the occasional gold coin. That day your mother escaped, she had twenty-five gold coins with her. Her chance at a better life. And a life unencumbered by Arcania for you."

I'm overwhelmed by how much Spencer did for Mom. The lengths he went to in order to protect her.

"I don't know what to say," I murmur, overcome by emotion. "Thank you for saving my mom. And me."

Shadows cloud his eyes. "But ultimately, I didn't save Ava because I believe Cora found her and if so, she has her sights set on you."

CHAPTER 40
CORA

T HEN

IF LOSING Ava the first time around had devastated me, this time my pain is unbearable. More so because when I return to Arcania I have to pretend like everything is fine. I have to pretend that I didn't witness my only child dying when struck by a bus. I have to pretend like I didn't meld into the crowd and run away so I wouldn't be blamed for her death. I have to pretend like I haven't just killed another member of my family, no matter how inadvertently.

I remember Harlan ranting about Arcania's curse one day and now I wonder if I'm tainted with it, too. I scoffed at the time, putting it down to the ravings of a lunatic because Harlan's obsession with finding the compass consumed him, but with the deaths on our collective consciences, maybe there's something to it after all.

I can't get the image of Ava's expression as she stumbled out of my head. She'd been aghast and repulsed by me reaching out to touch her and, in her effort to avoid it, she'd fallen into the path of that bus.

To be so abhorrent to my daughter, to listen to her accusations that I wouldn't have stood by her and that's why she cut me out of her life hurts so deep I'll never recover. As if the guilt I caused her death isn't bad enough.

A small part of me wonders if I can make amends by establishing a relationship with Lucy. I want to reach out to her so badly there's a permanent ache in my chest where my heart once functioned. The same heart that's now shattered because Ava and I will never have a second chance.

But I can have one with Lucy if I approach her carefully. She'll be grieving now and not in the right frame of mind to embrace a grandmother she obviously knows nothing about. From what Ava said, she'd left to protect Lucy, and that means my granddaughter is unaware Arcania or I exist.

It's particularly difficult to pretend in front of Spencer. I had to research the wellness centre on Long Island where I supposedly went for two days because he asked me about it at length, as if trying to catch me out in a lie.

And when he goes through the guests arriving tomorrow, I wonder if he knows more than he's letting on. Because there are two couples checking in and one single.

Lucy Phillips.

There are a million Lucy's in the United States, but my heart pounds as I look her up. No social media profiles, which is a red flag in itself if Ava wanted to keep them hidden. But I find a grainy photo of a Lucy Phillips at a librarian convention held late last year, and it's her.

My granddaughter.

Who's coming to stay.

I assume she's seen Ava's tattoo and linked the *vegvisir* to Arcania, but why has she taken this long to reach out?

She'd be twenty-five, plenty of years for a curious girl to want to know more about her extended family. So the fact she hasn't called or visited before now means she doesn't know.

Any of it.

She arrives the next day at dusk. I watch her from my office window, my pulse racing at the thought of our impending meeting. I need to play it cool. Find out how much she knows. Lead gently into our familial bond.

She stares at the taxi's tail lights for a long time as if wishing she could leave, and I know then she has no clue we're related. If I was in her place, I'd be dying to meet my relatives, to have support as I grieve. But Lucy is trudging up the path toward the house as if Arcania is the last place she wants to be and my heart aches for this poor girl who's now motherless.

Because of me.

I meet her halfway to the house, I'm that eager to meet her. She's the spitting image of Ava, and me, but if she sees the resemblance between us, she doesn't show it. We exchange pleasantries and I welcome her to Arcania. I give her the usual spiel and we head toward the house to check her in when I notice she's not following.

Instead, her gaze is fixed on the *vegvisir* emblem emblazoned on the back of my tunic.

She's definitely seen the tattoo on her mother's sole.

"Our logo is something else, isn't it?"

"It's distinctive."

"The only one of its kind. My husband's ancestors were from Iceland, so you'll see a lot of Nordic influence in Arcania. We use Norse mythology and symbolism in a lot of our treatments, too."

She wants to ask more. I can see it in her eyes. Which proves she doesn't know who I am and has come here to investigate her mother's links to this place, just as I assumed.

The thing is, I can't have Lucy poking around too much. She may discover a lot more than I want her to. And she'll figure out by the lengths her mother went to in order to escape Arcania, we have secrets to hide. She'll blame me too, just like Ava did.

I'll give her a few days, get to know her better, before revealing small clues that will lead her to the conclusion that I'm her grandmother. The realization has to come from her, because if she figures out I know the truth about our familial bond and have been hiding it, she'll have more questions I have no intention of answering.

CHAPTER 41
LUCY

On the walk back to the mansion, Spencer tells me his suspicions. He knows for a fact, courtesy of travel receipts on the wellness center's computer, that Cora had been in New York City the day my mom died, and the day preceding it. So he's assuming Cora somehow discovered Ava was alive, where she lived, and pushed her in front of the bus because her daughter had betrayed her and was of no use as the future heir to her one true love, Arcania.

"And you think she's somehow grooming me for the role?"

Spencer nods. "It's the only explanation why she'd harm your mother."

By his trembling hands before he shoves them into his pockets, I can see now's not the time to poke holes in his theory. My grandfather—it's unbelievable to even think we're related—is seriously rattled and I want to placate him.

"If what you say is true, me leaving abruptly will only anger Cora and she'll still come after me."

His expression is pained. "Let me think—"

"Won't it be better if I confront her? Get her to admit she's toying with me. I mean, she already wants me to stick around and do her precious research, so if she knows who I am, maybe I can get her to admit the truth?"

He shakes his head. "It's too risky. I heard Craig and Demi checked out early, and now Jase and Cindy have too. So you're the only guest here and confronting Cora will be foolish."

I try not to let my fear show. If Jase and Cindy have left too, I'm alone in a remote mansion with a lunatic and others I'm still not sure I can trust.

"With all due respect, my entire life has been a lie. My mother, who I adored, kept secrets that now, according to you, may put me in danger. So I would rather face this thing head on than run away, not knowing the truth."

"You're just like her." Tears fill Spencer's eyes and I'm mortified I made this kind man cry. "Ava was brave and headstrong, too."

Sadly, that's not the mother I remember. To me, she was timid and reclusive and quiet, and it kills me that my mother was so affected by Cora and the cult-like life she must've led.

"Daphne's around, and you're here now, so if I confront Cora in the dining room or one of the other public spaces, she'd never harm me in front of potential witnesses."

For all my bravado, I can't forget the strange happenings in this house. It's like the mansion's walls throb with malevolence and Cora is its mistress.

If Cora feels threatened by me, what will she—and the house—do?

It's silly, because a house can't hurt me, but I've seen

too much since I've been here, heard too much, to discount the possibility of otherworldly things at play.

"This isn't a good idea," Spencer mutters as we reach the house. "But you're right. Secrets have festered here for far too long and if you want to be truly free of Arcania, confrontation may be the only option."

Filled with equal parts relief and foreboding, I say, "No time like the present. I'll ask her to meet me for a coffee in the dining room in ten minutes."

I can see Spencer's still conflicted, so I reach out and lay a comforting hand on my grandfather's shoulder. "It'll be okay."

By his wan smile as he covers my hand with his, he's not convinced.

That makes two of us.

~

"Have you had a chance to consider my offer, Lucy?" Cora accepts the mug of coffee I hand her. "I think it'll be a wonderful opportunity for you."

I wait until she sits at the table and I choose the seat opposite, grateful for the wide expanse of wood between us. "I already have a job, so don't need the opportunity. And the only reason I'd accept is to discover the truth about my mother's links to this place."

I rest my forearms on the table and lean forward slightly. "After all, it's the only reason I came here, to see why Ava Reynolds, my mother, or Ayva as you pronounce it, had Arcania's emblem tattooed on her foot."

There it is. Cora's tell. Her eyes widen and she grips the handle so tightly the mug jolts and coffee sloshes onto the table.

She knows.

Knows about Mom, knows about me.

"Nothing to say, Grandma?"

Cora's face collapses in on itself. There's no other description, for her eyes seem to shrink back in her skull, her cheeks hollow, and her mouth droops.

"I didn't want you to find out like this," Cora whispers, her head rocking from side to side like she's trying to dislodge heinous thoughts. "I wanted you to love this place as much as I do, then I'd reveal the truth."

Stunned by the games she's been playing—and even more flabbergasted that we're related—I say, "Which truth? That your cruelty drove my mother to fake her own death to get away from you? That you somehow found us? That you killed her?"

"I never killed Ava!" she yells, and I jump. "True, I discovered your whereabouts by sheer chance. A guest mentioned I had a lookalike who worked at the Lower Manhattan Library and it sparked hope. I've always wondered if Ava faked her death, so I researched the library online but couldn't find a picture of you, so I headed to New York on a whim. I was shocked when I saw you at the library, how much you looked like Ava, so I followed you home. When you opened the door, I saw your mother..."

Cora clutches at her chest in an overly dramatic gesture I don't buy for a second. "I was distraught and overjoyed at the same time. I wanted to run to your door and bash it down. But I knew Ava wouldn't want to see me like that, so I waited until you left for work the next day and slipped a note under her door asking her to meet me near Central Park. I thought a public place might reassure her. But when she left the house, I couldn't wait, so I approached her and we talked a little. We hadn't finished when she walked away from me and she was about to cross a road. I tried to get her attention, and she startled and..." Her lower lip trembles. "You know the rest. I'll never forgive myself for it."

I want to believe her, I really do, but this woman must've terrorized my mother in the past to make Mom run to protect me, so I can't trust a word she says.

"So you didn't push her in front of that bus?"

"Good heavens, no." Her eyes filled with tears and either Cora is a brilliant actress or she's genuinely sad. "Losing Ava devastated me. The only way I could function was to throw myself into ensuring Arcania thrives. It saved me at a time when I wanted to fling myself into the swamp."

I want to empathize, but I can't. If I had to choose between Spencer and Cora as to who to trust, it wouldn't be the latter.

"Why did my mother want to leave Arcania so badly she faked her own death?"

Cora blinks rapidly, and her tears disappear. "I've asked myself that same question ever since I discovered she was alive. We were a community here. Everyone loved the atmosphere we created."

When I arch an eyebrow, she clarifies, "Harlan, my husband, and I. After his parents died, we built this place into something special. A legacy for Ava to inherit. Losing her devastated me."

I want to say 'because you loved her or because you're so obsessed with Arcania you're desperate for someone to continue your work after you're gone', but I don't. I never expected her to open up like this and I want to keep probing for answers.

"So why didn't you approach me after Mom's death? And what would've happened if I hadn't come here?"

She gives a little shake of her head. "You were grieving, and I didn't want to intrude. I'd planned on giving you time, maybe a month or two, before reaching out. But then you booked here as a guest and I couldn't believe my luck, that I'd get to know you without the added pressure of you resenting me for appearing in your life at a time you wouldn't welcome me."

"That's a lot of assumptions you've made," I say, unable to quell the bitterness. "I don't like playing games, and everything you've just told me makes me feel like you're toying with me. Is that what your research offer is about? Making me stick around so you can mess with me some more?"

"Of course not, dear." She releases her grip on the coffee mug and starts wringing her hands before quickly lowering them beneath the table. "I thought spending one-on-one time together while you research would give us an opportunity to bond before I revealed our connection."

I want to ask about Spencer and how he fits into all this, but she hasn't mentioned him and that means she's unaware we're in cahoots. I'd prefer to keep it that way, because whatever lines she's feeding me, I can clarify with him.

"I know this is unorthodox, Lucy. How we've met, how you've discovered our familial bond. But now that you know, I would like it very much if you stayed on at the end of this week and we spent some more time together."

She sounds genuine enough, but there's an avaricious glint in her eyes. She sees me as a replacement for Mom, a pawn she can move at will. Too bad for her I'm brilliant at chess and I refuse to be checkmated.

"I can see you're not convinced, Lucy, but please give me a chance. I want a do-over with you because I failed Ava so badly. We can help each other. You just have to trust me." Her gaze is almost maniacal, and I suppress a shiver. "Arcania will be yours one day and if we can work together to find the golden compass, our legacy will live on for generations."

So that's her endgame. The compass. And everyone along the way has been a means to an end. She doesn't care about me. Spencer's right. Arcania is all she values and she'll do anything to preserve it.

I want to fling the accusation in her face. I want to call her out for being a callous liar who'll do anything and say anything for her precious Arcania.

But I don't.

Because I know what I have to do now.

I must leave and get as far from this toxic place and my twisted grandmother as I can.

CHAPTER 42
CORA

ow

EXCITEMENT FIZZES in my veins as I make my way through the tunnel leading to the chamber. This has been a big day. Lucy knows the truth and rather than absconding as I expected, she's contemplating my offer to stay at Arcania. It's more than I deserve, especially when she'd been suspicious about my role in Ava's death.

But she'd listened to my explanation and accepted it as the truth, so I'm hopeful we have a chance at establishing a genuine relationship. I crave that.

When Ava had flung those accusations at me, how I hadn't been there for her when she needed me most, they'd hit home. I'd done my best, but my fear of Harlan had tainted our lives and perhaps if I'd made a stand earlier, none of this would've happened.

I can't change the past, but I can do a damn sight better

in the future and that's what I'm hoping to do with Lucy. She reminds me so much of her mother, beyond the way she tilts her head and gnaws on her bottom lip when she's thinking. She has an innate gentleness about her that calls to me, and I'll do everything in my power to make up for the mistakes of the past in a do-over with my granddaughter.

As for how Lucy found out about me being with Ava when she died, Spencer must've discovered I'd been in Manhattan and made assumptions. I should be angry at him, but I can't summon the energy. Especially when he's asked me to meet him down here because he thinks he's finally discovered a vital clue that will lead to unearthing the compass.

Magnus and Helga, then Harlan, and for the last decade me, have wasted countless hours in search of the artifact that will bring glory to the mansion, put Arcania on the map, and ensure our family legacy for decades to come. While I understand why Ava changed her surname when she fled, I'm hoping Lucy will legally change back to Medville when the time is right. If she comes to love Arcania as much as I do, I'm confident she'll do it.

That's what today is about. If the legacy of Arcania can live on through Lucy long after I've gone, I'll do anything to find the compass.

When the tunnel gives way to the small cave, I see the chamber door open.

"Spencer?"

"In here," he calls out, and I enter the chamber, suppressing a shiver.

I've only been in here once before, when I suspected Harlan might've been trapping our missing workers here. It would be the perfect place because when the tide comes in, they'd be swept out to sea without a trace.

Back then I'd found nothing and the mere thought of the ocean entering this chamber is enough to give me goose bumps.

The darkness is all-consuming, the air dank, and as I reach out blindly I encounter a jagged rock that's damp to my touch. The tide must've gone out recently and while it should inspire me with confidence, it doesn't. I know how quickly the tides change here. It's an anomaly locals have whispered about for years, a silly superstition that the souls from the shipwrecks scattered along this coastline are angry and demand justice by causing inexplicable tide surges.

I've never paid much attention to those tales, but now I'm here, a hint of something otherworldly ripples over me and I shudder.

"Spencer, I can't see a thing," I murmur, the chill in the air piercing my cotton jacket, and I tug it closer around me.

"Let your eyes adjust, then you'll see it. The clue. I can't believe it's been here all along." His voice is coming from my right and as I take a step toward it, I hear soft footfalls behind me.

I spin around, still blind. "Spencer?"

A door slams and a light flicks on, illuminating Spencer's face in the small glass porthole set high in the door.

His expression is apologetic, but his eyes are wary, like he doesn't trust me.

Fear crawls over my skin like ants, and nausea clogs my throat as I break into a cold sweat.

He's trapped me in the chamber.

My legs are jelly-like as I make my way to the door and

try the small round steering wheel that mimics the larger one on the outside.

It doesn't budge.

Dizziness swamps me, my heart pounding so hard I can't breathe. My torso trembles and I drag in deep breaths, willing the spots dancing before my eyes to disappear. The last thing I need is to pass out.

Once my breathing and heart rate are under control, the wooziness passes. Spencer is a kind man. He's stayed by my side for over four decades, so whatever game he's playing won't last. Perhaps this is payback for what he thinks I did to Ava? Whatever his rationale, I need to talk him into letting me out of here.

Keeping my voice steady in an effort not to clue him in on my terror, I say, "If this is a prank, it's not funny."

He's stony-faced. "I'm sorry, Cora, but it's the only way to get the truth out of you."

"What truth?" I snap and rattle the wheel on the door again. "Let me out so we can have a civilized conversation."

"No. Because I can't trust you."

My stomach clenches at his contemptuous expression. "You've known me for forty-four years. You've stuck by my side all that time. And now you say you can't trust me?"

He's conflicted. I see it in the way his gaze shifts, but not before I glimpse a flicker of remorse. "I initially stayed for you, to make sure Harlan didn't harm you like the others. But then I stayed for Ava."

"So Harlan killed those employees who disappeared?"

"I don't know how he did it exactly, probably drugged them and trapped them here. But yes, he boasted about it one night when he ingested hallucinogens. The lunatic was proud of getting rid of his parents, too." He shakes his head. "He was a cruel man and to this day I can't believe you married him rather than leaving with me when we had the chance."

Surely Spencer isn't doing this because he's harboring the resentment of a jilted lover? Doubtful, but my belly knots with regret at the many mistakes I've made. No good can come of rehashing the past, but I know one thing: I'd do it all again to protect my daughter.

"I did it for Ava. To give her the life I never had." My lips press together to refrain from saying so much: how I know now he's right, that we should've left together when we had the chance, that I never should've married Harlan, that I should've grown a backbone sooner and stood up to him. "Surely you can understand that?"

He nods, his eyes downcast. "I can, because that's why I stayed. To protect her." When his gaze locks on mine again, I see defiance. "And it's why I helped her fake her death."

My mouth drops open, and he continues. "She came to me, desperate, and I had no idea what to do. I knew what Harlan was capable of and he'd go ballistic when he found out. Then I found a corpse on the beach and what I had to do became clear." He blanches, at odds with his resolute tone. "I severed a finger, then told Ava of my plan. I gave her money, told her to stay off the grid completely, and get as far from here as possible without telling anyone who she was and where she came from." He jerks a thumb over his shoulder. "She went through the other tunnel."

I can't believe this. The one man I thought I could trust has lied to me for decades. And while I admire his protectiveness toward Ava, I can't forgive him for decimating my life in order to protect hers.

"What other tunnel?"

"One you don't know about that leads to an alcove about three miles away. I left a car there registered to an

Ava Reynolds, because she wanted to keep her first name to make things easier."

Stunned by his duplicity, I say, "So you've known where she's been all this time? You watched me mourn my only child like some sicko ghoul?" I thump the reinforced glass with my fist, fury making me shake. "How could you do that to me?"

He has the audacity to shrug. "It wasn't about you. I would've done anything to protect my daughter. Something you should've done if you had the guts to stand up to that bastard Harlan."

My anger deflates as quickly as it came. "You know?"

"I've always known Ava's mine," he snaps, a vein pulsing near his temple. "I was in love with you, Cora. It means I studied you at length. Every facial expression, every smile, every sigh. While you were busy trying to impress the Medvilles, I was watching you."

"There's a name for that. It's stalker."

A mean response because I knew how Spencer felt about me, but I lied to him, regardless. I'm not proud of what I did, deliberately sleeping with Harlan to ensure everyone thought he was the father of my child. And the lengths Spencer went to in order to ultimately protect Ava proves how much he loved his daughter despite me telling him otherwise.

I've made so many mistakes. I have to live with so many regrets. It's sickening, but I vow to do better with Lucy.

"You were into me too." A frown slashes his brow. "That's how I knew Ava was mine because you targeted Harlan hard in the weeks after we slept together, like you needed his money, which meant you had something, or someone, to protect."

I could lie to him again, but what's the point? I must get out of this chamber and to do that, I need him on my side.

"You're right. She's yours."

Anger sparks his eyes. "Thanks for the confirmation. Not that I need it. I've been a better parent to Ava than you ever were." His glare is laser-like, skewering me with hatred. "Did you kill her?"

"Of course not. I'm not a monster."

He pauses, as if begging to differ. "Lucy told me what happened, but I'm not sure I believe your story."

Tears burn the back of my eyes at the memory of what I did. "It's the truth. I just wanted to talk to Ava, but she wanted nothing to do with me. I went after her and in an effort to get away from me, she stumbled on the curb and fell in front of the bus." Sorrow squeezes my chest at the loss of my daughter and yet another tiny white lie I have to tell. "It was horrific."

"So horrific you came back here and pretended like you hadn't even been in the city?" His tone is scathing. "Can you see how that might make me suspicious?"

I want to yell that I don't care what he thinks. Ava is dead and all the retributions in the world won't bring her back. But I need to tread carefully because now I've confirmed Lucy is his granddaughter, who knows how far he'll go to turn her against me?

I never would've thought this gentle man, who knows about my ocean phobia, would trap me in here in some warped attempt at getting me to spill the truth. Placating him is the only way I'll get out of here.

"You mentioned Lucy told you what I said to her about Ava's death. Does that mean you're chummy with her?"

"She trusts me, because I haven't lied to her from the start." He presses his face closer to the glass as if trying to get a closer look at me and his upper lip curls in a sneer, as if he doesn't like what he sees. "Why did you do that? If you knew who she was, why not tell her when she arrived?"

At last, a question I can answer honestly.

"Because I wanted to give her time to get to know me." I sweep my arms wide. "To fall in love with Arcania as much as I have. This will be her legacy and I didn't want to force the issue—"

"I can't believe this. You're as obsessed as Harlan was." He scowls. "Is Arcania all that matters to you?"

I want to deny his accusation, but there's been enough lying. "Arcania is everything to me and knowing I have family to inherit it has made me tread carefully with Lucy. I don't want to scare her off."

"Like how you scared off her mother, you mean?"

"I loved Ava!" I yell, pounding the glass with my fist again. "But she abandoned Arcania and I don't want Lucy to do the same, which is why I've made sure she falls in love with this place as much as I did."

Spencer's eyes widen and I realize that in the heat of the moment, I've said too much.

"What did you do?"

My heart sinks, but he's lived at Arcania longer than I have, so I assume he knows what Magnus and Helga did to new arrivals to keep them happy.

"Do you know about the micro-dosing?"

His glower is formidable. "What the Medvilles did to newcomers? Yeah. Those weekly parties they threw for the employees where they'd spike the punch with whatever drug they had handy..." He trails off as realization dawns. "You've been drugging Lucy?"

His skin is mottled, his eyes so wide I can see the whites. I don't blame him for being enraged, but he doesn't understand. I'll do anything to ensure Lucy stays with me here and gets what's rightfully hers.

"Not drugging exactly, but micro-dosing with hallucinogens in her water bottles and smoothies, then projecting old videos of Ava onto the walls so she thinks the house has otherworldly qualities and her mother is tied to it somehow."

I'd always wondered if Harlan insisted on the hideous green wallpaper during the initial revamp because the walls became a green screen and he wanted to torment me with supernatural phenomena somehow, but I'd never been more grateful for it when I first hatched my plan to make Lucy stick around.

I doctored old videos of Ava growing up and projected them into Lucy's room some nights; I used an old projector to superimpose lights on the orchard one night, I even made a bold move and projected during our meditation session when Craig and Demi left the room.

With every trick I employed that didn't scare Lucy away, I knew she was becoming invested in solving the mysteries of Arcania. Offering her a chance to research the history was my finishing touch because I knew she wouldn't pass up the opportunity to learn more about Arcania and Ava's links to it.

A genius move, one I hope will lead to us spending a lot of time together and solidifying our tenuous bond. Ava may have betrayed me by faking her death and running away. I won't let Lucy disappoint me.

"I did it because as long as Lucy is curious about her mom and how much Arcania meant to Ava, she will stay."

He's appalled, his face twisted in disgust. "You honestly think that by duping your granddaughter into thinking this house has magical qualities she'll stick around?"

I tilt my chin up and stare him down. "I'm willing to do whatever it takes."

When he continues to glare at me with disgust, I say, "Don't pretend like you're innocent. If you knew about the spiked punch, is that why you gave me some the night Ava was conceived?"

He reddens. "I didn't know until years later what the Medvilles were doing. I'm not a monster who drugs unsuspecting people."

Unlike me, he wants to say. I see the condemnation in his glare, but before I can say anything else, the first slap of icy water submerges my ankle. I look down, not computing why the ocean is lapping at my feet.

When the reality sinks in, I scream.

CHAPTER 43

LUCY

'm sitting in the foyer when Spencer finds me.

I didn't want to be anywhere near that tunnel and that creepy underground chamber while he puts his plan into action.

When he first told me about trapping Cora in the chamber to get her to confess to murdering my mother, I thought he was as crazy as my grandmother. What would a confession achieve? Even if she admitted the truth, would I have the emotional fortitude to press charges? To prosecute one of the few family members I have? And where's the proof unless Spencer records their conversation? A recording that could be questioned in court because the confession was coerced under duress.

But Spencer was adamant about learning the truth and after much deliberation, I gave in. Not because I believe Cora is guilty of murdering my mom, but if I learn the truth and she's innocent, I may foster a relationship with her. It will take time, because I don't like how she's lied to me from the start, pretending she didn't know me, but I'm willing to try if she is.

Mom had her reasons for fleeing but now she's gone, I want to get to know Cora and make up my mind. Foolhardy? Maybe, but there's something about this house I'm drawn to and I want to know more about my extended family, no matter how dark the secrets are .

I hate the idea of Cora being trapped in that tunnel and chamber. It had given me the creeps, so I don't think it will take long for her to confess, especially if she shares my fear of the ocean, as Spencer said.

The thought of being trapped in that chamber with the tide coming in... I shudder and rub my arms.

"Are you okay?" Spencer asks, resting his hand on my shoulder briefly before sitting alongside me on the purple velvet chaise lounge.

I nod. "How's it going down there?"

He grimaces and swipes a hand over his face. "It's not my finest moment, trapping her like that, but it's the only way to get the truth out of her."

"Has she said anything?"

He hesitates, dejection radiating off him. "You won't like what I'm about to tell you but I'm so sick of this place and its secrets."

When he doesn't elaborate, I reach out to him and lay a comforting hand on his forearm. "Tell me."

He clears his throat and blows out a breath before speaking. "Cora has been drugging you."

Shock makes my jaw drop. "What?"

"Micro-doses of hallucinogens, in the water bottles in your room and in your daily smoothies, then using digital technology to project videos of your mother as a teen in some warped way to make you think this house has supernatural links to her in the hope you'll stay to discover more." He shakes his head. "It's sick, her obsession with this place."

So that explains those visions of my mom on the walls, and the sound of her voice, but what about the rest? The warmth of the doorknob and the key fob in my hand, the oppressiveness of the walls closing in on me, the startling awake in the middle of the night because of a presence?

I know it's crazy, but a small part of me had hoped Mom had been trying to reach out to me, to tell me something. But Cora's been perpetuating a sham and I've fallen for it. As for the rest, it's probably a figment of my overactive imagination, fueled by hallucinogens and missing Mom.

I can't believe Cora's played on my emotions. Why didn't she just tell me the truth from the start?

"I'm assuming she put the diving suit in my room too?"

"Probably. Everything she does is to find the gold compass because she believes the legend about appeasing the Norse gods." He barks out a laugh devoid of humor as he reaches into his coat pocket. "Ironic, because I found this years ago and nothing around here has changed."

When he opens his hand, a burnished gold compass with the *vegvisir* embossed into it sits in his palm.

"You found it?"

He nods. "About a decade ago. I've been diving the shipwreck since I first arrived here over forty years ago and came upon it by sheer chance."

"Why didn't you tell Cora?"

"Because I wanted to save it for you. In case anything ever happened to your mom." He takes hold of my hand and presses the compass into it. "This is your insurance policy. It's worth a fortune and whatever happens to me or Cora or this house, you'll always have it."

The compass is hot to my touch and when he releases my hand, there are tears in his eyes. "The only reason I stayed in this godforsaken place all these years is on the off chance you would show up one day and I could give you this. I thought your mother might tell you the truth eventually, and you'd find your way here, but when you first arrived and didn't seem to know anything, I waited." His expression is somber. "Considering the lengths Cora went to, maybe I shouldn't have."

I stare at the compass, glowing softly in the lamplight.

My legacy.

And the one thing that has driven my grandmother to do unthinkable things.

"Thank you," I murmur, wrapping my arms around my grandfather in an impulsive hug.

He squeezes me tight for a moment before easing back. "What are you going to do if Cora confesses to murdering your mother?"

"I don't know."

It's the truth, because I have no idea if a confession will bring me peace or not, or whether seeing her locked up for her crime will appease me.

"Well, I need to know what really happened," he says, standing. "It may sound heartless, but I'm going to wait until the tide is in about chest-height, because she'll definitely want to get out of the chamber then."

It seems so barbaric, torturing Cora by using her fear of water to gain a confession. It would be my biggest nightmare. Then again, if she pushed my sweet mother in front of a bus so she could control me in some warped plan to groom me as heir of Arcania, she deserves the terror of being trapped in that chamber with an incoming tide.

"Do what you have to do," I murmur, and with a last squeeze of my shoulder, Spencer is gone.

CHAPTER 44
CORA

ow

I DON'T KNOW how long Spencer leaves me here. I lose track of time because I'm blinded by panic. My body has shut down. I'm numb as the cold seeps into my muscles, then my bones, the terror chilling me as much as the frigid Atlantic.

As the water level rises, so does my abject horror.

How could Spencer do this to me?

I cling to the doorknob, twisting it to no avail. The *vegvisir*, the symbol of hope and power, mocks me. I have given up so much in my quest to make Arcania great again.

My husband. My daughter. My sanity.

As the tide rises from my calves to my hips to my waist to my chest, I know I will die here.

It's inevitable.

I'm cursed, like all the Medvilles before me, those

ancestors Harlan told me about, the ones who gave up everything in search of the compass. His parents, who he murdered so he could be the sole beneficiary when he found it.

But I'm nothing like them. I didn't let greed get the better of me.

Didn't you?

I ignore the tiny voice in my head. It's my conscience, and now's not the time to acknowledge the lengths I've gone to.

A ghostly face appears in the window set into the door and I lose my footing, almost submerging. Water sloshes over my chin, onto my lips, and the taste of salt makes me gag.

"Ready to tell the truth?" Spencer asks, his face a stony mask. But I glimpse a flicker of regret in his eyes and I need to play on that sympathy.

"Spencer, please. You, me, and Lucy can be a family." My teeth are chattering, but I'm immune to the cold now. My entire body is frozen and hypothermia will set in if he leaves me here any longer.

I'll do anything to escape.

Including confess to a murder I didn't commit if it comes to that.

"Lucy doesn't need family like you." His lips peel back in a grin that borders on maniacal. "I gave her the compass."

The cold must've affected my brain because I could swear he just admitted to giving Lucy the compass I've been searching for all these years.

"What?"

"You heard me. Lucy now has your precious compass." He taps his chest. "I found it ten years ago."

Shocked, I press my face against the glass separating us. "You know what that compass means to me, what it means for Arcania. Do you really hate me that much you'd let me continue fruitlessly searching all these years?"

Sadness darkens his eyes. "I don't hate you, Cora. But your obsession has made you immune to logic, and I held onto the compass on the off-chance Ava or her child returned here one day."

My mind's a jumble as I try to understand what this means. All these years, I thought that possessing the compass would appease the Norse gods. I allowed my superstition to rule everything, like Harlan once had.

But if Spencer's telling the truth, finding the compass has done nothing. This house is still oppressive. It still has a presence. It still haunts me.

"I can't believe you let me waste my time searching for it all these years."

His upper lip curls in a sneer. "I didn't 'let' you do anything, Cora. You've been blinded by greed."

I open my mouth to refute his accusation, but before I can speak, a surge of salty water fills it. Spluttering and panicked, I stand on tiptoes, belatedly realizing that while we've been talking the tide has risen further and is halfway between my chin and mouth.

I'm out of time.

"You need to let me out now, Spencer."

I tilt my head back to keep the water off my face because I know if I take another mouthful, I'll lose it completely and will drown before he opens the door.

"Not until you tell me—"

"Fine. I killed our daughter. I pushed her in front of that bus because I knew she was lost to me and I had another heir in Lucy. Is that what you want to hear?"

209

Our eyes lock and his fill with tears.

"You are the devil," he mutters, but he reaches for the door handle and turns it to the left to unlock it.

I weep in relief, but it's premature.

There's no clunk as the bolts slide into place.

Instead, the wheel spins.

He grapples with it, turning it left and right, and his panic rises with the tide.

I know when that door clicks, an underground drainage system will activate and the ocean swamping me will ebb away. Harlan had told me how this tunnel and chamber system worked during my first week here, like he'd been trying to impress me.

Ironic, that he killed so many down here and now I'll die the same way.

My greatest fear—drowning—has become a reality.

"Cora, I'm sorry, there's something wrong with the handle," Spencer yells, frantically grappling with the wheel, but it continues to spin uselessly.

There's no life-saving clunk.

No tide draining away.

No time left.

My body convulses as I know this is the end. I claw the door as my feet leave the chamber floor. I'm floating, out of my depth, out of options.

"Cora, I'm sorry..." Spencer's cries are lost as I submerge, and the terror shredding my insides consumes me.

This is my payback.

For murdering Harlan.

For killing my daughter.

Because in the split second before I lose consciousness, I finally admit the truth, albeit to myself.

Ava's complete disregard for what she put me through during our final confrontation triggered something in me and when she turned away like I meant nothing, I wanted to teach her a lesson.

I wanted to scare her.

I wanted her so frightened she'd turn to me.

I wanted her to need me.

Instead, I'd pushed her to her death.

And the one redeeming thought as I drift off is I'll finally be reunited with my daughter.

EPILOGUE

LUCY

Cora's memorial is small. The only people in attendance are Spencer, Daphne, Arcania's part-time yoga instructor, Nancy, the cleaner Babs, the beautician and massage therapist Moon, and me.

We bury her alongside Harlan and his parents in a tiny private graveyard at the back of the property that overlooks the sea. It seems fitting the burial is at dusk, when Arcania is shadowed in mauve and midnight, with dark colors and shadows that highlight its menace.

Because despite Cora's revelation to Spencer that she drugged me into hallucinating, I'm not convinced the house itself isn't evil. I feel it. The walls pulse with an invisible force, a low-level hum that manifests at the oddest of times. Too many have died within Arcania. Who knows what presence haunts it?

I'm not scared with Spencer now sleeping in the room

next to me, though I can't wait to leave. It's my family's home but I can't stay. I'm sad because despite what Cora did to harm people over the years, how she murdered her husband and daughter, a small part of me had been grateful to discover I have family beyond Mom and now that's been taken away from me.

As for my paternal family, Arcania kept lax records —for obvious reasons, considering staff kept disappearing—so there's no record of my father's surname and I have no way of tracing his extended family. Mom kept zero mementoes, so that'll be a dead-end too. It's a shame, because somewhere out there I may have grandparents, aunts, uncles, and cousins I'll never know.

At least I have Spencer. He's distraught. He blames himself for Cora's death. His guilt has aged him ten years since the night she got trapped in the tunnel's chamber. The lines around his eyes and mouth have deepened, his shoulders appear perpetually slumped, and his eyes lose focus at times.

He's been nothing but kind and protective of me since I first arrived at Arcania and I wish I could make this better for him. But if he stood by my grandmother for decades then couldn't save her, he must have deep feelings and nothing I can say or do will help.

I hope that over the next few weeks while I stay at Arcania to assist with settling affairs—namely, put the place on the market and hope a realtor can shift it fast—I can support Spencer in whatever way he needs.

I'm glad he's moving to Manhattan to be closer to me. It'll be nice to get to know my biological grandfather. DNA testing has proved it because while Cora assured Spencer he was Ava's father while she'd been trapped in that chamber, I didn't trust her not to say anything in an effort to escape and I wanted irrefutable proof.

It's heartless, how Cora robbed him of being Ava's father yet kept him around. He's told me how they had a secret affair for years following my mom's eighth birthday and I can't believe Cora played on his feelings for her. A small part of me is relieved he's free of her now.

He could've walked away from me and washed his hands of our familial mess, but he's committed to deepening our tenuous bond and I'm grateful. It makes me feel less alone in my topsy-turvy world.

I intend to bestow a sizeable chunk of the money from Arcania's sale to him. He deserves it after all he's done for me.

But I have to be careful.

I can't afford to lower my guard while spending time with Spencer.

I can never tell him how I tampered with the door to the chamber to ensure it couldn't be opened once the tide started coming in, ensuring Cora wouldn't live.

How her precious compass emblazoned on that door handle also signifies revenge and I made sure Cora got her comeuppance for brutally killing my mother.

How from the minute Spencer told me about his plan to lure Cora to the tunnel's chamber and scare her into divulging the truth, I'd known I couldn't settle for anything less than getting rid of my twisted grandmother.

Ironic that Cora ultimately got her wish.

I'm now the heir to Arcania.

And I can't wait to escape its tainted walls.

*Want to read a new shocking twist, this time from
Spencer's point of view?
Sign up for the exclusive scene here.*

If you enjoyed THE RETREAT, you'll love BANISH.

ALYSSA WOOD HAS *one week to annihilate her enemy and save
her soul.*

*After her ex-boyfriend dies and her mom's alcoholism sparks
yet another psychotic episode, Alyssa flees her small hometown of
Broadwater and heads to New York City to stay with her
bohemian aunt—a Wicca High Priestess.*

*Alyssa revels in the anonymity of a big city and her new life.
Her grades improve, she makes a good friend, and meets a new
guy, the sexy geek Ronan, a saxophonist who prefers jazz to pop.
But her newfound peace is obliterated when she glimpses a dead
body in one of Ronan's music clips—and she's the only one who
can see it. Worse, Alyssa recognises the body that has been
murdered a week into the future.*

*Alyssa doesn't believe in the supernatural, despite her fami-
ly's Wicca background. But as the secrets start to unravel, evil is
closer than she thinks and she's powerless to stop the inevitable...*

PROLOGUE

TIME TO PUT the past to rest.

I edged towards the door leading to freedom and
clasped the knife, its weight reassuring in my hand.
Ignoring the pain in my palm where it had accidentally

sliced as I'd bolted to escape, I focused on the kitchen doorway and waited. Waited for him to come after me.

A shadow fell across the doorway and using both hands I raised the knife, holding it high and extended, like a Samurai.

He stopped at the kitchen door, malevolence radiating off him. He raised a finger and drew it across his throat in a slow, deliberate slit. "You're dead."

He stepped into the kitchen, the absence of emotion in his icy glare almost as terrifying as the slow curling and unfurling of his fingers. I had no doubt those fingers would end up wrapped around my throat.

"Give me the knife, bitch."

The insult didn't freak me out as much as the uncanny timbre of his voice; how much he sounded like my dead ex. Wish I'd noticed the resemblance sooner. Would have saved me the hassle of carving up his ass. For there was one thing I was sure of: I'd managed to endure this god-awful week so far, no way would I go down without a fight.

My trembling fingers convulsed around the knife, gripping the handle tighter as I lowered it to chest level. "Make me."

The eyes of the guy I'd once trusted glowed with hatred. A second before he lunged at me.

I feinted to the right, slammed my hip against the sink and cried out in pain.

He laughed, a chilling sound that had me scrabbling faster as he came straight for me.

I swept the glass on the draining board to the floor and dodged to the left.

He kept coming.

Panic clogged my throat as I rebounded against the wall, hard enough to rattle the crockery in the dresser. I should have baulked, should have screamed, should have run. Instead, an inner strength I hadn't known I possessed snapped its leash. Clawed its way to the surface, howling for freedom.

He must have seen something in my expression because he hesitated.

I didn't.

I screamed my fury, desperate to lash out.

Unable to rein in my rage, I slashed.

READ BANISH NOW!

Acknowledgments

For those of you who've read my domestic suspense novels, you know how much fun I had writing them.

So when someone suggested I explore a gothic storyline, I couldn't resist and the creepy Arcania was born.

Four decades ago in my teens, I loved getting swept away to haunting mansions and their secretive inhabitants within the pages of books by Victoria Holt and Daphne du Maurier. It's been way too long since I've read those books and writing The Retreat has reignited my love for gothic. I hope you enjoy it as much as I did while writing it.

My thanks to the following people:

MaryAnn Schaefer, for her unending support and excellent proofreading, especially picking up all my 'Aussie-isms'. I'm so appreciative of you.

Debbie at The Cover Collection for creating the perfect cover to encapsulate my story. I love the colors, the picture, the font, absolutely everything!

The Author Hive for their collective wisdom.

The members of my Readers' Room on Facebook, I love how you're always willing to help with plot points. Invaluable.

The fabulous readers who've signed up to my newly created Suspense ARC Team. Your speedy reading and reviewing is immensely important. Thank you.

Soraya and Natalie, always only an email away for support.

Martin, here's another story where the husband gets his comeuppance, LOL!

My parents, my rocks.

My beautiful boys, love you times infinity.

The readers, bloggers, bookstagrammers, BookTokers, booksellers, librarians, and everyone in the bookish world who helps promote and sell my books. Thank you.

FREE BOOK AND MORE

Read Nicola's newest feel-good romance **DID NOT FINISH**

Try the **BASHFUL BRIDES** series

NOT THE MARRYING KIND

NOT THE ROMANTIC KIND

NOT THE DARING KIND

The **CREATIVE IN LOVE** series

THE GRUMPY GUY

THE SHY GUY

THE GOOD GUY

Try the **BOMBSHELLS** series

BEFORE (FREE!)

BRASH

BLUSH

BOLD

BAD

BOMBSHELLS BOXED SET

The **WORLD APART** series

WALKING THE LINE (FREE!)

CROSSING THE LINE

TOWING THE LINE

BLURRING THE LINE

WORLD APART BOXED SET

The **HOT ISLAND NIGHTS** duo

WICKED NIGHTS

WANTON NIGHTS

The **BOLLYWOOD BILLIONAIRES** series

FAKING IT

MAKING IT

The **LOOKING FOR LOVE** series

LUCKY LOVE

CRAZY LOVE

SAPPHIRES ARE A GUY'S BEST FRIEND

THE SECOND CHANCE GUY

Check out Nicola's website for a full list of her books.

And read her other romances as Nikki North.

'MILLIONAIRE IN THE CITY' series.

LUCKY

COCKY

CRAZY

FANCY

FLIRTY

FOLLY

MADLY

Check out the **ESCAPE WITH ME** series.

DATE ME

LOVE ME

DARE ME

TRUST ME

FORGIVE ME

Try the **LAW BREAKER** series

THE DEAL MAKER

THE CONTRACT BREAKER

ABOUT THE AUTHOR

USA TODAY bestselling and multi-award winning author Nicola Marsh writes page-turning fiction to keep you up all night.

She's published 80 books and sold 8 million copies worldwide.

She currently writes contemporary romance and domestic suspense.

She's also a Waldenbooks, Bookscan, Amazon, iBooks and Barnes & Noble bestseller, a RBY (Romantic Book of the Year) and National Readers' Choice Award winner, and a multi-finalist for a number of awards including the Romantic Times Reviewers' Choice Award, HOLT Medallion, Booksellers' Best, Golden Quill, Laurel Wreath, and More than Magic.

A physiotherapist for thirteen years, she now adores writing full time, raising her two dashing young heroes, sharing fine food with family and friends, and her favorite, curling up with a good book!

Made in the USA
Monee, IL
17 July 2023

39423720R00135